VICTORIA GRACE,
THE JERK FACE

VICTORIA GRACE,

JE^{THE}RK FACE

S.E. CLANCY

WhiteSpark

This is a work of fiction. All characters and events portrayed in this novel are either fictitious or used fictitiously.

WhiteSpark Publishing, a division of WhiteFire Publishing
13607 Bedford Rd NE
Cumberland, MD 21502

ISBNs:
978-1-946531-65-0 (paperback)
978-1-946531-67-4 (hardcover)
978-1-946531-66-7 (digital)

*For my mom: Thank you for loving me,
even when I insisted on plain cheeseburgers.*

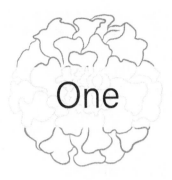

One

KEEPING A FIRM GRIP ON MY HANDLEBARS, I SWIVELED my head toward the music…and my dream car.

My morning had failed spectacularly. My Twenty One Pilots poster mysteriously fell from the wall during the night and left a massive crease across Tyler's face. The janky water heater broke for the third time in a week, and my shower hovered a degree above glacial. And although I rarely wore eyeliner, the tip I tried to smear across my eyelid broke, and I ended up with a lovely scratch that resembled a raging case of pink eye.

Now I waited at the light on a bike, next to a car I could never afford. I expected a thumping bass line or twanging country, not "Bohemian Rhapsody," the song that always weaseled its way into my mom's playlists. But the guy in scrubs behind the wheel looked like he was trying to recapture his teenage years with custom dance moves.

Through the clouds, the sun glinted off stock chrome bumpers and down the curves of a 1967 red Mustang convertible. Even the rims were original. This was exactly what I needed. But I could be flexible. It could be a 2016 Mustang with air conditioning and leather seats, with no complaints from me. I only lacked the funds to own anything other than the blue ten-speed cruiser I got for Christmas three years before.

Back when I was fourteen, it was the best Christmas present a girl could ask for, complete with a miniature license plate bearing my name: TORI. The ridiculous matching helmet I'd outgrown was stuffed somewhere in the dark corners of my closet, along with the license plate. Three years later, the bike was my only form of transportation, when I couldn't beg a ride from my mom. Maybe MamaBear didn't feel my pain of being one of the only juniors at Butte High School without a car. Had the man who was biologically my father paid child support, I might already have owned a ride. But that's another story.

The only highlight of the morning? It was Friday.

After the Mustang sped away, I pedaled on the back roads to school, fleeing the traffic backups and aggressive drivers jockeying for position to drop off their kids. It resembled a colossal competition of car Jenga.

If I could make it through the day without seeing Zane and his posse, I'd be fine. It was easy enough to disappear in school, but this type of day would land me straight in the path of the stereotypical, majestic captain of the football team.

My pocket chirped as I snaked the cable through my bike tires. I spun the lock closed and fished my phone from my jeans.

Mads: I'm sick today. So sick.

If my friend was sick, I was a natural blonde. I envied Madison's ability to manipulate her parents into more three-day weekends than what I imagined most homeschoolers enjoyed.

What tropical disease did you catch?

Her absence narrowed my lunchtime choices to one option: eating with a book on the steps outside the cafeteria, hoping the September clouds overhead wouldn't dump rain.

Most kids I knew were acquaintances, not friends. After moving to Redding as a sophomore, the jump from a tiny mountain community high school to one with over eight hundred students was more than a culture shock. There were groups and sub-groups—a hierarchy. Some thrived in their groups. Even fewer floated between more than one clique. But I was content on the fringes, friendly to all and provoking none.

Mads: Malaria. Or Zika.

I swiped the message into oblivion and sprinted to Spanish class. One more tardy and MamaBear would ground me for all eternity. The bell rang as I slid through the doorway.

My whole point of existence at Butte High was to play basketball, earn enough money to buy a car, graduate, and get community service credits for a college scholarship to anywhere other than Redding. Forget a boyfriend from the shallow pond of people who grew up and were related. Every day marched in the same boring way. Too many cowboy jocks, too many triple-digit summer days, and too few things to do for those unfortunate souls stuck in my age group. The limited options included sneaking out to parties thrown by upper classmen with their how-do-you-like-my-new-hair-color girlfriends, or going to the movies. And since I happened to work at one of the two multiplex theaters, I couldn't wait to come up with my half of the cost of a car. It was my ticket out of far northern California after I graduated.

Rain splattered the windows during my Creative Writing class, before the lunchtime bell. Great. Not only would I be shoving food into my mouth in the hallway, I'd be fleeing to the library and into the territory of the self-righteous scholars of the school. They littered the tables in the hushed room, taking turns giving me the stink eye whenever my chair groaned against the floor. Who made the decision to install cheap woodgrain flooring in a library?

I hated reading James Joyce during lunch, but it was necessary. I wanted to spend an hour obsessing over Mustangs or random pictures on Instagram and Pinterest, but I had a paper due Monday and needed to keep my phone charged for my shift after school.

After lunch, my locker jammed. Of course. I trekked to the office and waited for Carl the janitor to escort me back to the deserted hallway. I wasn't his favorite person. My locker seemed to be possessed with a sticking lock, no matter how many times he fixed it.

When I made my way into American Lit, three minutes late, Mr. Long expressed no sympathy, even with the note from the office.

Either my teachers were sadistic or they'd simultaneously experienced worse mornings than mine, because by the end of the day, I ended up with homework in every class. Sweet. Instead of complaining of nothing to do between shifts at the theater and my Saturday babysitting job, I'd be slaving at my laptop. Exactly how every seventeen-year-old dreams of spending her weekend.

At least I hadn't lost my mind over trying to find a homecoming dress, like a majority of the girls in the hallways at the final bell. I never expected to be asked. Wasn't a big deal. I may have mentally drooled over the way Zane's shirts seemed to be painted across his torso, but in no way did I want to be anything other than a girl with a secret crush on him. I'd taken enough basketball bus trips the previous year to realize Zane wasn't anything other than eye candy. Yummy, black-haired, blue-eyed, sculpted-muscles, selfie-obsessed eye candy.

Another red Mustang blasted by me on the ride from school to work—as if it weren't enough to avoid potholes and hobos while weighted down by nine million pounds of school books in my backpack. I'm pretty sure the world plotted against me the entire day. Damp from the drizzled ride when I arrived at the theater, I hurried upstairs.

After changing into dry black pants and a dull white T-shirt with the theater logo peeling off of the back, I checked the mirror in the employee bathroom for ruined mascara. I twisted my wet, stringy hair off of my face with bobby pins. But the rebel in me left the tiny stud in my nose because my manager wasn't scheduled to work. A new superhero movie had opened earlier in the day, and it would be a night of hustling from one empty theater to another to clean the perpetual deluge of popcorn and dodging the diehards who stayed to obsess over the credits.

I fired off a message to my mom before I headed down to the lobby, a clash of neon signs over black and white tiles.

At work. Off late. Rocky Horror showing at midnight.

MamaBear: Oof. Be safe. You have dinero for dinner?

Yup. Fast food is life.

MamaBear: Let me know when you are off.

Okie dokie.

The sigh escaped automatically as I trudged down the purple-carpeted stairs. Not everyone could have such a glamorous life.

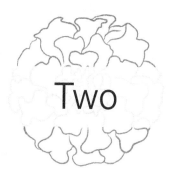

Two

THE ONLY WHITE CHRISTMAS I'D EVER SEEN WAS ON television and the internet. I had never tasted a chestnut, and open fires were illegal in Shasta County. MamaBear's cheerful note on the bathroom mirror the next morning, declaring, "98 days until Christmas," hardly conjured up visions of decorations or Nat King Cole's album that MamaBear would have on repeat during the entire month of December.

All I could think of was the assignment from youth group at church.

The scalding shower relaxed my muscles, beckoning my eyelids back down. Wednesday night, Pastor Matt said that teenagers were generally expected to underperform in life. We wanted things to be easy. He'd challenged us to do something hard, to step out of our comfort zones before Christmas. I thought it was a great lesson—right until the moment the youth group deadline reminder arrived, decorated with a smiley face on MamaBear's sticky note.

Thoughts of the Christmas deadline floated down the drain with my shampoo. My mind fiddled with the balance I had to earn to come up with the down payment for the car that MamaBear and I agreed upon. I was close.

A Mustang was out of the price range. Sure, I'd probably end up with a ten-year-old beater, more-than-likely-gold-colored foreign car, but it'd be mine. My choice of music would rule the stereo. I could prop a ridiculous piña colada-scented tree near the console because hanging it from the rearview mirror would obstruct my view. My luck, if I even hung it once, I'd get a ticket and that would mean no car. One of the downsides of having a cop for a parent.

Conditioner rinsed down my back when my phone growled on the counter. MamaBear was working the swing shift, eleven in the morning to eleven at night. It was her favorite shift, when all the "fun stuff" happened. She was probably checking to make sure I was awake. Instead of sending her a text as soon as I was up when I flopped out of bed near ten in the morning, I'd stumbled straight to the bathroom. I'm a naughty child.

After wrenching off the faucets, which had a tendency to drip incessantly if not forced shut with Herculean strength, I snaked my arm out of the curtain to retrieve the towel. Of course, it had fallen from the peg. I pulled it up from the floor, and an acrid odor hit my nose right before I dried myself.

"Trio!" I screamed into the otherwise-empty apartment. Stupid cat had peed on the towel while I showered. Sure, she was cute when she wanted to snuggle, but this was outrageous. She had a fully automatic self-cleaning litter box. The cat was a jerk, even if she only had three legs.

Naked, I rushed a few feet to the linen closet in the hallway and then back to the safety of the steamy bathroom, the fan humming in the ceiling. Out of habit, I'd already hung my clothes in the bathroom. Nothing like having your mom scare you into a routine with reminders like, "I handled a break-in today where a woman was showering," or "There was a fire downtown and the man had to jump out of his window—butt naked." Taking my clothes with me to the tiny bathroom was a small piece of insurance in case of an emergency. Heaven knows it would probably be my mom who would be dispatched to find her nude daughter crawling out the window to escape an ax murderer.

Once fully clothed, I swiped the fogged mirror and scrubbed

the clean towel back and forth across my hair, making it look even more asymmetrical. My phone growled once, then twice. Most people mistakenly thought it was a clip of Hulk roaring, not the snarl of a grizzly bear. I had no problem teasing my mom. After all, I happened to be her only cub and the target of her protectiveness.

I sent my reply, along with a smiley face. Emojis never hurt.

Sorry. Showered first and Trio peed on my towel.

MamaBear: I trained her to do that.

Nasty. PB&J then babysitting at the Branches. Work after. Off at 10.

MamaBear: See you then, kid. Love ya.

Some days, we'd have entire conversations in emojis, out of sheer fun and determination to see who would break. Happy to say, I'd never lost.

Turning my reflection one way and then the other, I breathed a sigh of relief. My skin decided to cooperate and there was no need for makeup, other than mascara. I'd ignore my freckles today.

Ugh. My boss would be working, so out came my nose ring, leaving a tiny hole that resembled a blackhead. The joys of a working stiff. I deposited the towel into the laundry basket on top of the one Trio had christened.

In the kitchen, I crammed a PB and J sandwich down the hatch. A quick refill of my filtered water bottle, and I was out the door to the babysitting job, a fifteen-minute bike ride from our apartment.

After I pedaled up the steep asphalt to the Branches's wrought iron gates, I punched the call button, trying to catch my breath and sound normal, instead of wheezing.

"Hi, Tori." Michelle Branch, attorney-at-law, chirped through the impersonal speaker. My mind never let her title drop after seeing it on late-night television, especially after I met the name-brand attired woman at church. I waved to the miniature camera at the keypad, which I didn't have the passcode for. No big deal—trust me with your kids but don't give me the gate code.

I pushed my bike through the ornate gates. The oversized stained-glass doors yanked open, and three-year-old Zach barreled down the stamped sidewalk, yelling my name over and over. Six-year-old Jack followed, hands buried in his favorite green plastic Hulk fists. After my first job at the Branch house, I swore I'd never tag my kids with rhyming names.

I barely had time to prop my bike next to the front door before I was dragged by one tiny hand and a Hulk fist into the "every-ceiling-is-vaulted" home. Michelle, as beautiful in person as she was in her commercials—and even more likeable than her silly television monologue—walked down the hallway while securing her hair with bobby pins.

"Leave Tori alone!" She chastised her sons by voice tone only. I wasn't sure if the two boys ever received parental discipline.

"The boys haven't had lunch yet," she said, "but there's plenty of food in the fridge. Oh, we are going to be late! It's my fault. I should've asked for you to come sooner. But they can't start without the guest speaker."

The guest speaker she referred to, her equally model-like husband Daniel, trotted down the carpeted stairs. "Hey, Tori." He flashed a toothpaste-ad smile.

"Hi, Dr. Branch. I'll get the boys' lunch started." Zach deposited his skinny butt onto my left Converse. "My shift at the theater starts at 4:30."

"No problem." Dr. Branch herded his wife toward the door.

I guided the boys to the doorway behind them, and we waved like trained seals while they sped off in a blur of a silver Mercedes.

Following an abbreviated lunch of canned organic raviolis, the clock sped by, assisted by the two animated boys. I played Black Widow to their Captain America and Iron Man, glancing at the enormous grandfather clock whenever I "died."

My stomach knotted as it grew closer to 4:00, then 4:15. I'd never been late. My manager didn't tolerate tardiness or downtime. As much as I wanted the money from babysitting, I couldn't lose my job. I paced to the window between toy retrievals until the chimes from the driveway sensor sounded and the garage opened. My teeth snapped together.

"I'm so sorry!" Michelle pressed folded bills into my hand.

I wadded the money into my pocket. "It's okay." Grabbing my bike, I sprinted through the gates as they swung closed. Helmet snapped tight, I flew down the hill, praying no cars would pull out from their pristine driveways. The lights worked in my favor. There was barely enough time to lock my bike into the rack in front.

"Hey, Rosie!" I called to the girl in the ticket booth. I scampered into work before she had time to call back through the microphone.

My I.D. beeped into the computer as my apple-shaped manager, Mr. Bolt, huffed around the corner. He narrowed his eyes at my hideous black pants and not-exactly-white work T-shirt. I hated the dress pants and had lobbied for jeans months ago. Since then, I was subject to Mr. Bolt's imagination that I'd try to sneak in a pair of jeans for a shift.

He shoved a lime-green T-shirt at me. "These just came in for the new release." The wretched neon top was a slight improvement over the required dingy white shirt. I sometimes wondered if corporate desk jockeys needed to embarrass the workers through forced clothing choices to keep the turnover rates high. My opinions aside, I slipped the T-shirt over my own, grabbed a walkie-talkie, and walked down the long hallway toward the ticket taker.

Aubrey adjusted her earpiece as I nodded a hello and squinted at the schedule. She and I shared a small sense of accomplishment, being the only girls on the theater crew. A firm believer in medieval patriarchal societies, Mr. Bolt loved to trap new girls in concession positions. Aubrey and I slogged our way through oily popcorn buckets, customer complaints about candy prices, and changing soda boxes. We advanced to cleaning spilled popcorn, customer complaints about the theater temperatures, and changing trash bags.

Midway through my shift, I spotted my church's youth pastor beckoning to me across the tiled lobby.

Pastor Matt was a guy who tried entirely too hard. His voice pitched up with enthusiasm whenever he returned from conferences, geared with new things to teach us. He wasn't horrible. A couple of the girls fawned over the single and eligible Christian youth pastor. It made my stomach roll, in a bad way. I mean, boys our age who were decent were few and far between, but Pastor Matt was a bit outside our range. It'd be like a gross news story.

But I felt like an outsider, preferring the green recliner in the high school room while everyone else scrambled for the blue couch or bean bags. I basically went because MamaBear went to church; it was therefore expected that I go to youth group.

The other kids weren't outright rude to me, but they conveniently forgot to ask me to non-youth group parties or get-togethers. However, their lack of notice allowed my super-spy stealth abilities to secretly drool over Greek-god-like Zane and Hunter, his dark-haired, handsome sidekick.

Eyeing Pastor Matt, I stowed my sweeper against the wall and made sure there wasn't any stray popcorn stuck to my belly. A quick hello and I'd be golden. The trick was to make it speedy, or I might be stuck in a conversation rehashing the youth group's camping trip to Whiskeytown Lake. The one I didn't go on because I was working.

"Hey. What are you going to see?" I asked the obvious question, but I was partially curious as to his taste.

"Zane should be here any minute. We're going to see that new spy movie."

I arched my eyebrows to hide the part of me that kinda died inside at his news. "I didn't know you guys hung out."

Pastor Matt slurped his soda through the straw and laughed nervously. "Well, I certainly didn't expect him to text me, but here we are."

I hummed an ambivalent response, glancing around for his

missing movie partner. Although Zane probably had no intention of anything beyond a friendly greeting, I didn't want to let him see me. Ever. I'd rather dream about our conversations than actually have one.

"Oh, I brought this in case I ran into you." From the depths of his red fleece zip-up sweater, Pastor Matt removed a gaudy purple paper. "It's an extra copy of the flyer from last Wednesday."

Mentally, I concurred with his observations Wednesday night. He wanted us to be what God created instead of what people expected. Personally, I didn't have time between work and school.

"Oh. Thanks. I gotta get back to work now." With expediency that would have impressed Mr. Bolt, I jammed the paper into my pants pocket and hustled to clean the bathrooms.

One would think, with all of the popcorn I'd made, burnt, and thrown out, that I would be repulsed by the unnaturally yellow pieces of fluff. But with a free container offered on breaks, I redeemed my allotted freshly popped snack and retreated upstairs for my thirty minutes after Pastor Matt's movie started. With any luck, Zane would never see me in such fashionable attire.

I'd forgotten about the paper until it poked my thigh as I sat at the employee room table. With twenty-five minutes to kill, I scanned over the list of "hard things" to do: volunteer to read to children at the hospital, habitually visit an elderly person, sign up for hours at the local teen crisis pregnancy center, and on and on. His whole list was thoroughly out of my comfort zone. And none of it interested me. Mouth full of oiled popcorn, I folded the paper and returned it to the safety of my work pants.

At the end of my shift, there was nothing quite as comforting as a quick flash of headlights. With sluggish steps, I thrust my bike into my mom's open car trunk.

"Spawn." Her face was lit by the dome light, devoid of makeup, and her hair seemed more black than brown in the dull glow. For once, I didn't care that she was in her Disney pajamas.

"MamaBear." As soon as I plunked onto the passenger seat and fastened my seat belt, my head dropped to the window. Eyelids drooped closed, no effort needed.

When the engine turned off, I jerked awake and struggled to unbuckle the belt.

"Go inside. I'll grab your bike," she said.

I walked to the apartment floaty, dream-like. My brain was pulling me to the down comforter on my bed, but I needed to wash the stench of gum remover from under my nails.

With as little effort as was necessary, I chucked the folded flyer onto the kitchen counter. I was sure my mom would see it the following morning and declare them all too dangerous for me because she didn't trust her daughter in the big, bad world with complete strangers. Sometimes, having a MamaBear worked in my favor, although it was a killer for the social life.

The next day, my eyelids barely stayed open for the late Sunday service at church. Once home and fed, I immersed myself in my History paper.

A flappy noise pulled my attention to my open bedroom door. Mom walked into my room, waving the flyer like a flag of surrender, Trio twisting around her ankles. Honestly, I'd forgotten all about the penned purple peril.

"Did you pick one?" Her eyebrow shot up.

I scrunched up my face. "Huh?"

"Which one did you pick?"

"Which one what?"

"How many ways do you want me to phrase it, Tori?"

"Well…" I laid my pen down, eyes glued to the flyer, while I scrambled for a response. "I wasn't sure you'd allow me to choose. I wanted to run it by you for permission first." Lame, lame, lame, but doable.

"Alrighty. Then my choice is number two. It'll also help out with your community service credits for the quarter."

My eyes rolled toward the ceiling before I let out a frustrated sigh. So unfair. I didn't particularly like old people. They wore polyester pants and smelled funny. The white-haired ladies at church didn't approve of my chain ear cuff and nose ring. I could get my community service credits other ways. But I kept silent—I knew better than to argue. She still held the proverbial keys to my future car.

"Fine." I dropped my gaze back to my homework. This was going to be a colossal waste of my time.

"I'll get ahold of the retirement home near your school and see if they have paperwork you need to fill out." I could hear the smile in her chipper voice.

MamaBear retreated from my doorway, and I returned to my paper, trying to put the darting thoughts of wheelchairs and Velcro sneakers to the back of my mind.

Later, I remembered to pray and asked the Lord to have MamaBear choose a different task or put the brakes on it altogether. Yes—I brought my requests and laid them at God's feet.

And He answered me.

In the morning, I found a freshly printed volunteer application for Willow Springs Retirement Home on the kitchen counter.

Well, amen to that.

Three

I DILIGENTLY FILLED OUT THE APPLICATION FOR WILLOW Springs, knowing it'd be worse to drag my feet or resist.

"If you want, I can drop this off before my dentist appointment." MamaBear waved the double-sided paper.

I shoveled oversized bites of waffle into my mouth and nodded, careful to return my gaze to the plate instead of rolling my eyes. So helpful, my mother.

Due to a random morning downpour, she was kind enough to give me a ride to school so I could miss the humiliation of the bus ride. Just thinking about the bouquet of body odor and cheap perfume made me beg. Most of the time, she caved, especially during the short winter months when I couldn't ride my bike. Otherwise, it was either my bike or the rolling metal zoo all the way to Butte High School.

Madison Dritz stood in front of the school and waved from under her umbrella. I catapulted from the door before the car barely rolled to a stop.

"What's up, chica? You never texted me back all weekend."

I wrinkled my nose at her grammar but didn't comment. She loved to poke my grammar police tendencies, especially when it came to using nouns like "text" as verbs. Our shoulders rubbed under the tiny umbrella.

"I had to work and babysit."

"Slave to society."

"More like slave to my bank account." I tugged open the door to the building with our lockers. Rainy days made me grateful that the school kept the lockers from the 1960s on the inside of the hallways. Two months later, and I'd be complaining about the stuffiness.

Madison flicked her umbrella closed and shook out her "yes-this-is-naturally-curly" blonde hair. "Blech. I hate the rain. I don't care if we're still in a drought."

"Is my mascara running?"

"Nope. Mine?" She squinted her green eyes.

"You use waterproof."

She laughed and twisted the combination dial on the locker next to mine. Coincidental locker placement last year and a well-placed Dr. Who sticker had made for a convenient conversation starter that grew into lopsided friendship—she'd talk and I'd listen. I didn't mind too much because I'd be going away to college soon, and she still hadn't made up her mind about anything other than going to the next school dance.

My phone growled. "Did you forget your lunch in the car?" Madison dipped her head from behind her locker door to wiggle her eyebrows at me.

"No. MamaBear is making me volunteer at an old person's home."

"Are you kidding me?" She slammed her locker and hugged her English book.

I retrieved my Spanish book and sent my own door crashing closed. "I wish I was."

Our pace quickened to the staircase and first period classrooms. "I hated visiting my great grandma when she lived there. It smelled worse than a boys' locker room," she said.

The first bell interrupted my sarcastic remark, and I fell into a conga line of classmates through the door of Spanish III. Technically, as a junior, I didn't have to continue the foreign language torture, but Miss Davenport was my favorite teacher. Her homework might've made me want to scream, but she was fair and had high expectations for her students. Plus, MamaBear pointed out pay bonuses for bilingual employees, and I figured, "*Me encanta el español.*"

School rules stated we were not allowed to look at our phones during class time. However, when mine growled again, I snatched it from my back pocket, hoping no one thought I farted. Mortifying. I flicked the switch to silent mode and saw there were now a couple of texts from MamaBear. They could wait. I didn't need detention.

In fact, I forgot all about those pesky messages until I dumped my Spanish book into my backpack and my phone flew out from its hiding spot under the open cover. With barely enough time to make it to History, I shoved the phone into my pocket once more.

A typical Monday, the day morphed into a flurry of busy nothingness.

Madison badgered me at our early lunch period. "You never answer your texts." She plopped down across the Formica tabletop. Her stepmom packed the best lunches: chocolate-hazelnut sandwiches, dill pickles, and cookies. Add in the green tea, and I drooled every time she pulled out her blue police box lunch pail. Yup—she carried a metal lunch pail, complete with a clip closure. Color me jealous.

"Sorry." My typical lame apology was easy enough. I dragged out my phone and cringed. Six messages from MamaBear, one from Madison, and another letting me know I had twenty percent off at the local second-hand clothing store.

I gnawed off a corner of my turkey-on-white sandwich and scrolled through the messages.

MamaBear: Turned in your application.
MamaBear: Ollo?
MamaBear: Don't answer during class or you're grounded.
Mads: Check out Zane-a-licious. Mmmm.

MamaBear: Are you ignoring me?

MamaBear: You can't get out of it by ignoring me.

MamaBear: You should answer me before things go terribly wrong for you.

My fingers flew across the miniature keyboard.

Sorry. Forgot phone in backpack. Ask Madison. Thank you for turning that in.

"Zane-a-licious?" I scanned the crowded cafeteria for the man-boy in question.

Madison turned and searched with me, the two of us probably resembling a pair of owls. She knew about my crush on Zane Boston—chiseled body, flowing black hair, and church attendee. "He has on the tightest shirt under his sweatshirt today."

"How would you know?" I asked.

"Well, it was hot in English this morning. And I couldn't get a pic for you, sorry."

I nabbed a fudge-covered cookie as my phone screen lit up.

MamaBear: I'll pick you up after school and drop you off for an interview.

"Oh, kill me now." I sighed into the cookie before shoving the entire thing into my mouth. MamaBear was out to slay what little existence I had.

"What's up?"

"My mom is taking me to the old folk's home after school today for an interview."

Madison laughed so hard that delicious green tea leaked out of her perfectly shaped nose. She inhaled it too and coughed violently, and we became the center of attention in the cafeteria for an entire fifteen seconds, though it felt like an eternity.

I handed her a napkin. "Thanks for the vote of confidence."

"Is my mascara running?"

Secretly, I hoped it had. "Nope."

"Well, good luck with those geezers."

My apple was bitterm and I lost my appetite. "Who interviews to volunteer at a retirement home? What kind of questions will they ask? 'Do you know how to change an adult diaper?'"

"'Can you press a medic alert button?'"

"Say goodbye to my social life." I dumped my lunch into the paper bag.

Madison laughed again. "You don't have a social life." She stood and I followed. "You work, go to youth group, play basketball, and read like a librarian."

"Bite me."

"I'll have to put in my dentures first." Madison scooted off to her class with a small wave.

The afternoon flew. I walked a half block from the school to the hardware store where MamaBear waited. After I chucked my backpack into the backseat, I landed next to her with a huff. Maybe it would make her feel a little sorry for me.

"You're going to run out of oxygen," she said.

I wasn't amused. I hoped my sideways glare conveyed my sentiments.

"Sheila called me this morning and is excited to meet you. She's the manager at Willow Springs. She says the residents there love to see young faces." Her selling points were as sad and pathetic as my life right then.

"Okay." This was my pat response for things when I knew I *had* to answer but didn't feel like it.

"Well, it's close enough for you to walk home."

Whatever. "Okay," I said.

"Tori, at least try to be polite. Most of these people are stuck in there by family members who forget all about them. No one visits, no one calls, no one cares."

"I will."

"Thank you. Who knows, you may find someone you like." She pulled the car into the parking lot of Willow Springs. Although she was probably trying to encourage me, it almost felt as if she was dropping me off to pick a kitten. One that didn't pee on towels.

Right. "Thanks for the ride. I'll send you a text when I leave." I hopped from the car, and MamaBear quickly pulled away, like I'd have a change of heart and hang onto the trunk as she left.

The tan stucco exterior was nothing special. Its name was scrawled in calligraphy font on a vinyl banner attached to the metal railing. "We Treat Your Family Like Our Own." Doubtful, but I was about to find out.

Pushing into the foyer, a wall of smell punched my nose: urine, chemical cleaners, and something musty. I forced myself not to crumple my entire face and beelined it to the receptionist. She was right around my age and looked out of place with platinum-white hair, the ends dyed bright blue.

"Can I help you?"

"I have an appointment with Sheila," I said.

"Yeah, sure. Hang on a sec." She leaned forward and tapped the telephone. "Hey, Sheila. Your appointment is here in the lobby. Okay. Yeah…okay. Bye." She glanced up at me. If I wasn't mistaken, she felt sorry for me. "She'll be right down. You can hang out here."

My sweaty hands wanted to bunch up my sweatshirt, but I pressed them together to remain as still as my unmoving feet.

"Hi!" The exuberant greeting came from behind me. I twisted to see a smiling woman, hair piled high into a haphazard salt-and-pepper bun with a pencil holding it in place. She walked behind an elderly, hunched-over man who clutched his walker. "You must be Tori!" Her words even sounded like they were smiling. Did I mention she was smiling? Her body was as wide as her smile.

"Yup."

"Walk with William and me. He's nearly done with his lap. Aren't you, William?"

The hunchbacked man with a tuft of white hair didn't acknowledge her question. He plodded forward one unsteady step at a time.

And thus began my interview with Sheila. I alternately took

a step then waited for the pair to catch up to me on the ugly linoleum floor.

"Why do you want to volunteer here?" she asked, maneuvering her hand to brace William.

The first answer that popped in my mind was the "best" one—because I like elderly people. But in the twelve seconds I'd known Sheila, I knew she'd smell a lie like a fart in a car.

"My church youth leader challenged us all to do something hard. I was trying to get out of it, but my mom picked this one for me because it qualified for school community service credits." Once my lips started moving, they wouldn't shut up.

"And do you like working with the elderly?"

"No," I said, scratching the back of my neck. "But I've never really spent time with anyone old. My grandparents all died before I was born, except my Nana. And I was seven when she passed."

"I like your honesty," Sheila said with a laugh. "Let's get William settled, and I'll introduce you to your new friend."

Like an obedient puppy, I trailed the tortoise-like duo back to William's room. We passed women sitting on chairs in the hallway and nurses bustling from their station to different places. Each room we passed made me more and more nervous; I didn't have a clue how to even talk to an old person—sorry, "elderly."

"You seem freaked out." Sheila chuckled as she washed her hands.

"Pretty much."

"When I was in nursing school, working with the elderly was the worst part for me," she confided, once we were walking down a random hall. "I didn't have an epiphany or see a light out of the sky. I couldn't find a job in a hospital at the time and got stuck working at a care facility. I was miserable and mad. Funny how you want something and end up doing the opposite. But then again, I don't believe in luck."

"No?"

"Nah. It's Providence."

I found it kinda cool that she used the politically correct term for God.

"Here's Marigold's room." Sheila led the way into the studio apartment.

Marigold? What type of mom named a kid after bright, ugly flowers?

A thin, wrinkled woman sat near the window, practically swallowed by the brown armchair. Her snowy hair was short and straight, smoothed against her skull.

When she turned to see who'd come in, the old lady's face lit up in recognition.

"Miss Sheila! I'm so glad you've come!" She didn't rise but held up her hand, coaxing us closer.

Sheila took the frail palm into her own. "Miss Marigold Williams, this is Tori Weston. Tori, this is Marigold."

Marigold peeked up at me, her pale blue eyes filled with... expectancy? She kept Sheila by one hand and held the other out to me. Clueless, I gingerly grasped her gnarled knuckles.

"Is your true name Victoria?"

"Yes, it is." I deplored my name. It sounded snooty.

"What is your middle name?"

"Grace."

"Oh, like Princess Grace! You should be called Victoria Grace," she whispered. "It sounds like royalty."

Sheila giggled. I didn't know what to do since Marigold still held onto me.

"I'll leave you two ladies to get acquainted." With a smile, Sheila disappeared and left me holding the hand of an elderly stranger.

Marigold gawked at me as if I were candy or a prize. I maneuvered my body, while captured, to sit next to her on the edge of the low window sill.

"It's very nice to meet you, Victoria Grace." The way my name rolled calmly off of her tongue had the opposite effect as when it was spoken by an angry MamaBear.

"You too, Marigold."

"*Miss* Marigold. Mind your manners. I am your elder, by a few years." She chuckled at her own joke and finally released her grip. "If you would be kind enough to fetch the picture from on top of my bureau?" Her bony finger pointed in the direction I needed to go.

Returning with the black-and-white photo in a scrolling silver frame, I sat down again on the sill and tried to give it to her. She refused and pushed it back toward me.

"That's me, eighty years ago—almost to the day."

My mind stumbled. I would've never thought about her as a teenager, only as an ancient lady in an oversized chair; but in this picture, Marigold had dark pin curls tucked tight against her crown over her almond-shaped eyes and the angle of the camera revealed a short bob of unruly locks. I assumed she had a dress on from the fitted bodice and lace collar.

"Sixteen was a magical age. But I lied and said I was eighteen to get a job in Hollywood."

Quick mental calculations put her around ninety-six. When I glanced up, Marigold was smoothing the blue blanket over her legs. She used short, elegant strokes, as if she were frosting a cake. It mesmerized me.

Then she caught me staring.

"I was an assistant of sorts to a movie star back then. I promised her I'd never reveal her name. Some ladies need their privacy, even after they are gone." Her silver eyebrows arched upwards as she continued. "I would do everything from hair and makeup at home to cleaning her little bungalow and even her grocery shopping. No one ever thinks movie stars eat." Marigold's thin lips pressed into a smile that suggested she would reveal nothing further on the matter.

"That's crazy! At sixteen?"

"Why, of course."

I felt ridiculous that I'd even thought to utter the question aloud.

"You must've forgotten your history lessons, Victoria Grace. This was during the Great Depression. Every penny I earned that I didn't absolutely have to use was sent home to my mother. She worked at a fruit packing house in Loomis. After I left, she couldn't feed four mouths because my father had already passed."

"Your hair was cute." I diverted the conversation into a safer topic, handing the silver frame to her.

"Oh, that was quite a scandal!" Her high-pitched giggle was as comical as a ticklish toddler. "I saw one picture of Miss Amelia Earhart and it was enough for me. It actually helped me land my job. My mistress saw me and told me my hair was sassy. I replied Miss Earhart was my hero. I was trying to decide whether to buy thread and a needle to fix my clothes or to eat that night."

I cringed at the thought of what a disaster my clothes would be if I had to fix them myself.

"Did you get to meet lots of other movie stars?" I asked.

"Heavens, yes! Ever so many. Most were very nice folks. I would be her serving maid when she had small parties. It was funny to see them eating and laughing, carrying on like normal people while the rest of the nation struggled by on rations. I'd always keep the leftovers and eat them. That way, I could send more money home."

"Did you ever want to become a movie star?"

"No." Marigold drew out the single syllable for a few seconds before succumbing to a cough, which seemed to rattle her from the inside out.

"Can I get you some water?" The way she gasped for breath made me nervous.

After she feebly nodded her head, I filled the small glass from her bedstand. Shifting from one foot to the next, I waited until she gracefully sipped the entire glass down.

"Victoria Grace." She strained to rasp my name. "I believe I need to call our visit to an end. Would you let the staff know that I need to be returned to bed when you leave?"

I agreed and waved from the doorway. Something about the way Marigold coughed picked my brain like an itchy scab. After letting the closest nurse know her request, the wall signs guided me back toward the entrance. I popped off a message to MamaBear.

"Was it bad?" Sheila grinned from behind the front counter as I pushed the entrance door open.

"Not really. Marigold had a nasty cough when I left."

Sheila came out from behind the counter and motioned for me to walk outside with her.

"I'd be breaking the law if I told you what she is going through. If she chooses to share her medical condition with you, it's her call." Sheila's voice cracked with emotion, while she struggled to keep a smile in place. I waited for the other shoe to drop. "I know your visits will mean the world to her. She is completely alone."

I knew I'd be back the next day, despite the glorious gulp of fresh air once I was outside. Besides, I needed the credits in order to bump up my college scholarship chances.

Four

"SO, YOU DIDN'T DIE." MAMABEAR PUSHED A PLATE OF food across the kitchen countertop as soon as I slid onto the barstool opposite of her.

"Nearly did. It smells worse than my shoes after a game."

Ah. She was buttering me up by serving my favorite: homemade tacos with extra cheese, hold the sour cream, drowned in hot sauce. I was willing to bet there was mint chocolate chip ice cream in the freezer.

"You took the first bite, you pray," she said.

I swallowed the mouthful of deliciousness and mumbled a quick prayer. "Thank you for the food, thank you for the day, amen." Get food in my belly before I become a grumpy girl who gets grounded for being hangry. Like a crazy, foul-ridden basketball game, hunger always brought out my inner beast.

We inhaled our dinner. MamaBear removed the dishes and chucked my backpack onto the counter.

I glanced inside it and groaned. "I hate math."

She stretched to put a plate into the dishwasher. The sparrow tattoo on her left wrist sneaked out from underneath her watch band. "Sorry I can't help much in that department, kid. I barely passed it myself."

"It makes me cry." I didn't have much to complain about. I still pulled a 93.7 in the class, but it never seemed good enough for my nagging inner perfectionist, desperate for a full-ride scholarship far, far away.

"Not sure if a tutor would do you any good, since you technically have an A in the class. Quit beating yourself up." She shook her head and headed to the outside laundry room.

English was first. Always. It was easiest to do and put me in a good mood. Plus, creative writing was a bonus. Then Chemistry and Spanish. Algebra II, the bane of my existence, was last. By the time I'd pulled out my Spanish III book to study for the test, a bowl of mint chocolate chip ice cream landed within reach.

"Thanks, Mom."

"You never told me how it went at Willow Springs."

I dug into the ice cream and talked through a mouthful. "Met a lady named Marigold. She's about nine hundred years old." Brain freeze hit, and I squeezed my eyes tight. Served me right. "She worked in Hollywood for a movie star during the Great Depression."

"That's cool. Did she say who?"

My bowl was almost empty already. Sad. I needed to slow down when I ate.

"No. She said, 'Some ladies need their privacy, even after they are gone.' I doubt I'll ever know who it was." My spoon clattered into the last of the melted green goo. I wanted to lick the bowl, but it would be frowned upon.

"That reminds me," MamaBear said, grabbing her phone from the back pocket of her jeans. "Madison texted me. You're not answering her again."

"No, Mom, she *sent* you a text. Text is a noun, not a verb." My only hope was to correct my own mother instead of an entire generation.

"Hashtag, back off grammar police. It's in the online dictionary." She rolled her eyes in my general direction.

I pulled my phone from my backpack and scrolled through the six messages Madison had sent in the last half hour.

Mads: How'd it go with the cottontops?
Mads: R U there?
Mads: Answer me!
Mads: U grounded bro?
Mads: Toriiiiiiiiiiiiiiii
Mads: Please?

"Oh my goodness, Madison," I whispered before I jabbed a response back.

Decent. Homework. MamaBear present.

Little bubbles flickered back and forth across my phone's screen while she typed her response.

Mads: Gotcha. You finished Chem?

I knew where this was headed. She wanted me to send her a picture of my homework and knew I hated giving her the answers. I snapped a copy of my paper and sent it before the "you-shouldn't-do-this" voice in my head forced me to lie and say I wasn't done. MamaBear would be totally disappointed if she knew. Madison's lack of preparation was not my problem, but I helped her anyways because I couldn't fathom failing a class. I needed the grades to get scholarships. My dad didn't own a bunch of local fast food joints. I didn't even know what my father did for a living. Didn't really care.

Mads: UR the best! CU in the AM

Fingernails down a chalkboard. No matter how many times I teased or corrected her, Madison's text messages looked like an illiterate goat typed them, one hoof at a time.

By the time I slapped my Algebra book closed, my eyes felt like they were bleeding. "I'm tired." I shuffled down the hallway and into my room. My favorite pillow kept my face-plant onto the bed from hurting.

"I got called in for overtime tomorrow. I wanted a full three days off." Even without glancing from my super comfy position, I knew MamaBear was standing in my doorway. Trio meowed her disapproval.

"Sorry." I turned over.

Poor MamaBear. She rolled her head slowly around her shoulders. Overtime would give her a down payment on a house, but days off were nice too. I patted the side of my bed, and when she dropped down, I rubbed her shoulders until my thumbs ached.

Later, when I was all snuggly in my bed and drifting off to la-la land, alternating between visions of a classic Mustang or a new convertible (red of course, with Zane in the passenger seat), Marigold seeped into my head. My nose brushed up against the fuzzy blanket MamaBear gave me the year before, and I had the weirdest thought before dropping into oblivion:

Did Marigold have a fuzzy blanket that kept her warm?

———— ⊣ ∘ ├ ————

If Tuesday blew by like a motorist at a yellow light, Wednesday was like being forced to ride a cargo train with a heavier load added at every station. A group project was given out in Spanish, History assigned a massive report due by Friday, and English dropped an assignment on us that would be turned into a contest for judging. Chuck in the homecoming game and dance on Friday, and my little world of boring became a living, breathing organism of hurry-up-and-get-it-done.

I was picking through Madison's lunch when my phone growled.

MamaBear: I can pick you up at Willow Springs before youth group.

No. I didn't need another thing to do. I must've groaned or sighed, because I was suddenly the object of Madison's scrutiny.

"What? Your mom okay?"

"Yeah. I gotta go to Willow Springs after school." Maybe I could do my history homework there. Would Marigold be offended if I told her I had a deadline?

"That's nuts," she said, sipping her lemon infused water.

I looked across the table at Madison's gel-tipped nails and

expensive shirt. It wasn't fair. I had to work my butt off to pay for community college, and she would go to a state university because her dad would shell out money for everything. I doubt Mads would ever have to work a day in her life. She'd probably end up marrying a lawyer and live in a gigantic house with multiple maids and nannies for their one kid.

"It is what it is," I breathed, in equal parts to Willow Springs and my yin to her yang in life. Better answer the text to MamaBear on an upbeat note, no matter my sour mood.

Sounds good.

"You really aren't going on Friday?" Madison pushed a cupcake across the table.

"Nope." I hadn't been asked to the homecoming dance, nor was I going to ask anyone. "Besides, I don't have a dress."

Madison scoffed. "You can borrow one of mine." No doubt, she had a selection from attending dances at Butte and a few other high schools in Redding.

"Alas," I said. "Zane is taken and my heart is broken."

"Huh?"

A deep breath later, I ratcheted down the fanciful language. "Mads. I'm not going stag. And being the third wheel with you and Josh isn't exactly my idea of a great time."

"Please?"

"No. I'm working, anyway," I said, grateful for the shift.

"Fine. But if you find a date in a ditch, I've got your back and you can still borrow a dress."

I snorted my laughter.

Cue the afternoon sleepies in class after lunch. The final bell rang, and I nearly bolted out of the door.

Diligent and obedient on the outside, I raged against the injustice of my plight on the bike ride to visit Marigold. I needed over fourteen hundred dollars to get a car. At least then, I wouldn't have to fight a fifty-pound backpack as I pedaled. Heck, I wouldn't even have to pedal anymore!

There wasn't a bike rack at Willow Springs. Why would there be? The little old people living there didn't have anywhere to go. Keeping bikes could encourage escapes. I smiled at the thought of William teetering on a bike, Sheila running after him, as I pushed my cruiser into the lobby. The smell was as overwhelming as it had been two days before.

"Uh, you can put that right up against the wall." Blue-haired girl nodded to the space opposite of the front desk. "That way I can see it and make sure no one takes it."

"Thanks." I propped it up near a bank of empty chairs. "I'm Tori, by the way."

"Jamie." Her gaze dropped to what I guessed was her phone, tucked between some papers.

"Do, ah, you need to let Sheila know I'm here?" How did one keep track of hours for community service?

"Nope."

I waited for Jamie to glance up. It never happened. "I guess I'll head down to Marigold's room." Don't mind me. Just your everyday criminal disguised as a high school student. My bike was totally going to be stolen under Jamie's vigilant eye.

It was weird to see the shriveled and worn residents in various states of sitting and walking stop to wave at me. A few held out their hand, as if they wanted me to stop and take hold. I pushed toward the opposite wall, like a kid playing with opposing magnets. Please don't touch me, old person. I don't like strangers.

A few missed turns later, I finally found Marigold's room. I knocked on the frame of the open door after spotting her lean body in the armchair next to the window. She resembled a pint-sized elf.

"Hi, Miss Marigold." Manners. I remembered!

With more grace than I could possibly have after weeks of training, Marigold turned from the large window, her eyebrows arched high above her twinkling blue eyes. "Good afternoon, Victoria Grace. I trust you had a pleasant ride?"

Suddenly, I felt like I was in a formal interview. "I did. Traffic wasn't too bad." I stepped inside the doorway and dropped my backpack onto the short-looped carpet.

Marigold stretched to look around the foot of the bed at my deposited load. "Gracious. It sounds like you have bricks in there."

I nudged the backpack with my foot. "Just my books. I have history homework I need to tackle."

"Let's get the table set up for you then."

To my horror, she maneuvered her way into a standing position, swaying ever so slightly. Did she really think she was going to move a table in here?

"Wait," I said. "Where is the table? I'll get it."

Marigold hobbled forward in her lilac-colored half slippers before answering. "It's inside the cupboard there." She pointed to the sliding doors on the wall in front of her. "It's only a card table."

"I'll get it. You can…" My brain struggled to get the words right. "You can sit down. It's probably not any heavier than my backpack."

"Thank you, Victoria Grace. I'll find a tablecloth while you get that all set up."

Behind a cute little vacuum and next to shelves with matching blue towels and washcloths, the card table in question was propped against the wall. I carefully extracted the table, watching Marigold out of the corner of my eye as she inched tiny step by tiny step toward the drawers next to the kitchenette sink. By the time I snapped the legs into place and righted the table in front of her armchair, she was shuffling her way back with a white lace bundle.

"That is perfect. We can sit together. I'll put the tablecloth on and you can go see about finding something to sit on," Marigold said, unfolding the material.

I was nervous leaving Marigold to her task, but figured the quicker I got a chair, the sooner she would be safely back into her own lounger. And I knew where to find one. I made my way to the lobby and heaved a chair into my arms. Jamie looked confused.

"Can I borrow this?" I asked.

"I guess."

Permission granted, I hustled down the corridor, dodging bodies and questions again.

Marigold was comfortably seated by the time I arrived. Breathless and sore from the angle I'd carried the "borrowed" furniture, I nearly dropped the chair.

"Lovely," Marigold said. "Set it there, across from me, and we can get started."

Huh?

"You've got to work on your poker face, Victoria Grace." Wrinkles piled together when she smiled. "Who better to help you with your history than a woman who lived it?"

My cheeks felt like they were on fire when I grabbed my backpack before plopping into my chair. I'd been trolled by a ninety-six-year-old.

The brown paper bag cover on my history book was embellished with hand-drawn flags and stars—my pathetic attempt at art. I had taped a Chinese cookie fortune across the top: "Trust takes years to build, seconds to break, and forever to repair." The book landed with a thud on the lace tabletop.

"Oh, U.S. History." Marigold pressed one hand onto the tablecloth. "I definitely know that. Except for the Revolutionary War. I was still a baby then." She pulled her hand back to cover her lips, giggling.

"I've got a report on Reform, Prosperity, and Depression from 1918 to 1939 due by Friday. It's the beginning of the unit, and my teacher wants a summary before we start."

"Lucky for you, I happened to be alive during most of that time period," she said.

All I could think about were the choppy black-and-white movie clips Mr. Hammond showed us in class and that she was alive while they were filmed. "Holy cow! That is a really long time ago."

"Does this haircut make me look any younger?" Marigold pressed her hair down and angled her chin up.

My mouth popped open and closed, like a fish out of water, before a Cheshire grin crept up my lips. "I like you."

"The feeling is mutual, dear."

Five

WE WERE FINISHING UP THE BASICS OF THE DUST BOWL and I was well over my five-hundred-word minimum when my phone growled from my back pocket.

"What a peculiar sound." Marigold examined my bright green phone case when I set it on the table.

"It's the ringtone I have for my mom when she sends me a text message."

"Is that a bear?"

"Yeah. I call her MamaBear. She's a tad overprotective."

"As she should be. You are her daughter. You are lucky. There are plenty of girls who need a mother to protect them instead of ignoring them." Marigold sniffed and straightened. I could see the angle of her bony shoulders under the bulky sweater. "Answer your mother, Victoria Grace."

I swiped the phone screen.

MamaBear: Be there in 10

Room for my bike?

MamaBear: Will bungee cords and duct tape work?

Perfect. Food?

MamaBear: Bread and water

"She's on her way to pick me up for church tonight." After I put my laptop and book into my backpack, I smoothed out the wrinkles in the tablecloth.

"It's nice to see a young person go to church. Do you like going?"

Depended on the scenery, aka Zane and/or Hunter's presence. "Well, I go to youth group on Wednesday nights, and MamaBear goes to the service. It's not bad. Do you want me to put the table away?"

"Oh no. We will leave it here for next time, don't you think?" Her pale blue eyes glittered. Was she anticipating my answer? How was I supposed to say no? Besides, my cousin Nick said colleges really ate up community service hours for scholarship considerations.

"Okay," I said. "I'm not sure if I'll be by tomorrow, though. And I work Friday night."

"Other than bingo, my schedule is wide open."

I laughed before I dragged my backpack onto my shoulders. "I'll call ahead to make sure you're available." Although half of my brain wanted to give her a hug, the other half told it to pipe down. I settled for a dorky wave as I left.

Under normal circumstances, I would've thanked Jamie for guarding my bike. But her desk was empty, except for the giant handheld bell with the sign: "Ring for Service." At least no one had stolen my trusty blue ten-speed.

I rolled my bike down the wheelchair ramp, and MamaBear pushed open the hatchback on her car. As I swung the frame into the trunk, the tasty smell from inside made my mouth water.

"Oh, you made meatloaf!" Call me a freak, but MamaBear's meatloaf was something I never missed—I don't care if Madison made fun of me for eating it. Those onions had me scrambling for the front seat.

"And mashed potatoes and green beans. Seat belt. Soda is in the cup holder."

"You're the best MamaBear ever."

"Yeah, yeah, I know." She pulled out of Willow Springs and toward church. "How'd it go with Marigold today?"

I chewed through a mouthful of green beans. "It was actually good. Have a history report due by Friday and she helped me. It's the time period right before she was born and while she was growing up." Mashed potatoes—get in my belly.

"That's kinda cool. When was she born?"

"1920," I mumbled through my dinner.

"Whipper snapper."

"Well, it's perfect timing for me with this unit starting up. She remembers all the details about growing up in the Sacramento area. She left when she was sixteen, after her dad died, and lied to get a job in Hollywood." I shoveled in another bite of meatloaf. "She was the oldest daughter of six kids—four girls and two boys."

"Her poor father. I have one of you. I can't even imagine that many estrogen bubbles flying around a house."

MamaBear pulled into the church parking lot as I polished off the last of my food. I was stowing the plate near my feet when Zane trotted by the front bumper, tugging on a sweatshirt over his fantastic display of biceps.

Desperation hit. "Do you have any gum?" It's not like he'd actually talk to me on purpose, but if he happened to, I needed to kill the onion breath.

"Really, he's not worth it." MamaBear held out a pack of peppermint gum to me. I nabbed two pieces and ignored her comment. Hopefully, the aroma of Willow Springs had not permeated my clothes. Better safe than sorry. I sprayed the citrusy perfume MamaBear kept stashed in the center console. She only used it when a crime scene was overwhelming.

"Okay, bye!" I grabbed my phone and hightailed it to the youth group room. There was nothing worse than arriving and having someone occupying my favorite green recliner.

Which is exactly what happened that night.

Although I'm sure I tried to look bewildered at the brown-haired boy in my chair, I'm pretty sure I gave him the evil eye before grabbing a beanbag and slumping near the foosball table.

Who did he think he was, taking my chair? All long-legged and skinny, silently observing everyone who entered. He barely cracked a smile at Pastor Matt as the latter barreled into the room.

"Hey, Corbin! Good to see you!"

And like meerkats on the Discovery channel, we all swiveled our heads to stare at the fresh meat. Boys were sizing up. Girls were internally going down a checklist. I wanted him to get out of my chair.

"Everyone, this is Corbin Dallas. He moved to the area from Texas last week."

Oh my. I pulled both of my lips between my teeth and bowed my head. First off, a last name of Dallas, from Texas? And his parents had to be more nerdy than MamaBear to name their kid after a 90s sci-fi flick. A half-chuckle-snort escaped, much to my embarrassment.

I cleared my throat, my cheeks flaming. In the most nonchalant manner I could, I danced my gaze to Pastor Matt, the window, and then Corbin. Of course, he was staring right at me. Awesome. It felt like my face was in front of the popcorn machine at work. He leveled his brown eyes at me and cocked an eyebrow. Obviously, he knew that I had caught on to his dorky name secret. What he didn't know is that he was named after my all-time favorite movie, *The Fifth Element*.

"Has anyone started on their big project to do something hard yet?" Pastor Matt bounced from one foot to the other, stroking his trimmed beard. He was a total hipster, down to the rolled jeans over his leather lace-up boots. "Zane?"

"Nah. Haven't even had time to think about it with school and playoffs." Zane tucked his hands into the front pocket of his sweatshirt. Gotta keep those star running back hands safe.

Beside Zane, Hunter covered his boy-man beard with his hand to hide his smile. There was a type of fad going around with the football players, and a bunch of them were sporting hideous, patchy facial hair.

"Playoffs!" Zane said. They did a secret-football-player hand-shake-slap, straight out of a cheesy film you see at a rally to encourage teamwork.

"What about you, Amelia?" Pastor Matt started making his way around the room. Oh great. Here came my big reveal about spending time with Marigold. The closer he came to me, the more I wanted to "use the restroom."

Then, a miracle. Corbin was technically the person before me, all comfortably stretched out on my recliner.

Pastor Matt rifled through loose papers near the door and handed one to Corbin. "I challenged the kids to do something outside of their comfort zone. It's based on a book I read."

"Yeah, by the Harris twins."

Huh. Mr. New Guy was familiar with youth group ways and ploys. Good to know. And his Southern drawl was hypnotic, even if he was a dirty chair thief.

"Exactly! That's the flyer I made for them, if you're interested. It's not required, a little assignment I wanted to throw out to everyone before Christmas. Last Wednesday of the month! Grab your jackets and let's head to coffee."

Hurray for invisibility and diverted attention!

Admittedly, this was my favorite part of our youth group. We'd walk in a herd down to the local coffee shop, where Pastor Matt would buy us small drinks. I usually ended up walking near the pack of six to ten girls so I wouldn't be stuck talking to Pastor Matt about my trivial life. No thanks.

Stuck behind the gaggle of jabbering youth group kids bottlenecked to get outside, I was a bit shocked to see Corbin hold the door open for everyone, including me, the last one out.

"Thanks."

"Super green," he said with a smile. Well, hello, adorable dimple.

"Multipass." It was such a relief to have another movie-quoting dork. He could sit in my recliner this one time.

"Good to see someone around here with culture," he said. That drawl was impossibly deep.

"Eh." I pulled up the zipper of my jacket. "There's a camaraderie among those named after books, movies, and plays."

"Which are you a victim of?" Next to Corbin, I felt short, even though I was five foot nine. He was close to six foot six. Probably had a nice hook shot.

"Technically, a play. But it was turned into a movie, so the best of both worlds." I stopped and extended my hand. "Victoria from the musical *Cats*, better known as Tori."

Corbin latched on and gave a firm shake. There's something to be said about a dude who shakes a girl's hand like he means it instead of handling it like a wet noodle. "Ollo, guv'ner."

We ended up as the caboose to the pack of teenagers and rambling youth leader. My breath sent out puffs under the streetlights, and I regretted my thin jacket.

"Where do you go to high school?" Corbin loped to my right, closest to the street. Was it my imagination, or was there a weird squeaking sound coming from him? A ringtone?

"Uh, Butte. You?"

"I start there on Monday, technically. Friday I get a tour."

I heard the squeak again. "What year?"

"Junior."

"Me too. Sports?"

"Basketball," he said. "I don't play on school teams though. Teammates tend to get a bit freaked out by this." Midstride, Corbin tugged up his left pant leg. The streetlight glinted off a metal prosthetic shin.

"Shiny!" I blurted a quote from *Firefly* to hide my shock, since I'd never actually met someone missing a limb. Hopefully, he wasn't offended.

"Well, this one is. My spare leg is blacked out." Corbin dropped the hem back into place. No one ahead of us would have a clue.

"Wow," I breathed, not sure of what else to say.

"I'm kidding."

The youth group made its way to the coffee shop more than thirty yards ahead of us and were jockeying for line positions. By the time we arrived, an awkward silence had settled between Corbin and me. Did he want me to ask about his leg?

I gave the barista my order and found an ottoman that hadn't been taken by the pack. Corbin introduced himself, getting names of the others, as he made his way to the only unoccupied, highly uncomfortable wire chair—across the area rug from my seat. No worries, I'd slip into ninja mode and observe.

One by one, we were called up for our drinks. When I watched Corbin chat with Zane about basketball, my curiosity piqued when the former did not make the same display of his robo-leg that he had shown me. As the queen bee Shelby passed by him twice for her drink, my judgment narrowed when Corbin's gaze lingered on her derriere. Whatever. My butt was nonexistent. Guys like him and Zane were the real reason I never dated or even kissed. That, and my mom and her super strict rules. Her well-known occupation had an effect of cutting through the crowd, too.

"Wrap it up." Pastor Matt waved his hand in a circle, trying to round us up like a bunch of cows. Yee haw. At least I'd gotten a yummy peppermint white mocha from the deal. He had forgotten to ask me about the assignment, and I was in no hurry to remind him.

Everyone filed out and Corbin held the door again. Great.

"*Gracias.*" My manners would always rise to the occasion, even when I didn't feel like it.

"*De nada. Hablas español?*"

"*Poquito.*"

He launched into a full-on conversation in Spanish.

"I'm only in my third year." I could feel the heat flood my cheeks, despite the cool night, because I only caught bits and parts of his fluid message.

"I was saying that it's nice to have someone who speaks

Spanish. Then I asked what classes you're taking. Grew up with ranch workers, and I picked up Spanish along the way."

"A ranch in Texas. How very stereotypical of you," I said.

"I never was into the cowboy hats. But I do have boots."

Ahead of us, cell phone camera flashes lit up the sidewalk. Probably a flurry of selfies.

"We used to live out in the country in Oregon." I missed the wide-open skies at night, star constellations bright and far away from the glowing amber streetlights. I didn't miss the spotty cell coverage.

"Working cattle ranch, myself. Proverbial saying applies—I learned to ride before I walked." He half laughed, half pushed out a breath. "Although I was either with my mom or dad."

"How many acres?" I could totally show him I knew my country lingo, no belt buckle required.

"A little over six hundred, passed down over generations." He plucked his cell phone from his back pocket and flicked through pictures before passing it over. "That's the house my great-great-grandpa built."

Even on the tiny screen, the two-story, white-washed plantation house was impressive. Little black shutters outlined each window, and the porch roof was low slung, like a cowboy's belt.

"Is that your dog?" I zoomed in on the picture near the front door to a squatty black-and-white pup.

Corbin cleared his throat. "Sheba. She was the best cow dog my dad ever trained." He kept walking forward, never looking as I examined this picture.

I caught the fact that Sheba "was" the best dog and swallowed my next inquiry about her. "Pretty lil' thing." Best to go the safe route.

"Yeah. She's barely ticking at sixteen. Not going to make it much longer."

The squeak started again from Corbin, and I could only presume it was from his leg. I handed his phone back.

"How'd you end up moving to Redding from Texas?"

"Grandpa grew up here. Met Grammy while he was in the service, and they settled back in Liberty Hill, outside of Austin, when he got out of the army." Corbin didn't put the phone away immediately. He kept the picture of the house up, inspecting it as we walked. I stole glances as he stared at the tree, the front door, and Sheba again until he turned off the screen and held it in his massive hand.

We were nearly back to the church when I finally figured out a question to fill the silence. "Do you know what classes you're taking?"

"Not yet. There are some issues about transferring state to state and requirements. So, I guess that's what I'll find out Friday."

"Ah, you get to see all the homecoming nonsense."

"You going to the dance?"

My heart felt like he'd reached in and squeezed it. Why was he asking me about the dance? I swallowed hard before answering. "Nope. Gotta work. You going?"

"Nope."

"What are you doing your first Friday night in the exciting town of Redding, California?" Up ahead, I could see MamaBear visiting with a group of people outside the front doors of the church.

"Probably gonna see a movie."

Of course he was going to a movie. With my luck, I'd be seeing him sooner rather than later, rocking my attractive neon-green work shirt at the ticket podium.

Sucked to be me.

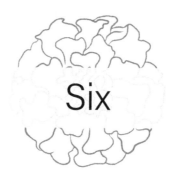

Six

"WHO WERE YOU WALKING WITH?" MAMABEAR HAD
the decency to wait until the car doors were closed before the in-
terrogation began.

"New kid, Corbin. He moved here from Texas. Junior. Starts at
Butte on Monday." The more information I fed her, the less likely
she was to ask me more questions. My gaze landed on said boy
moseying toward a white-haired woman who waved him over.

"Who's that?" MamaBear asked, putting the car in reverse.

"No idea."

"Looks like it could be his grandma."

"I don't know, Mom." Really. She was acting like I'd been on
my first date without her permission. I wasn't that stupid…most
of the time.

"He's cute."

I groaned. "Stop."

The entire ride home, I could tell she wanted to ask more
questions but kept them tucked away for later. It was the way she
took a deep breath in through her mouth, then exhaled through
her nose while drumming her fingers on the steering wheel.
Ironically, as her mini-me, I mimicked the same gesture. Still, I
was grateful she didn't push.

My phone vibrated in my back pocket, and I fished it out as we
parked in front of our apartment.

Unknown: Hey. It's Corbin.

Well, alrighty then. How would I play this? Try to be nonchalant or demand to know how he got my number? Maybe a combination of both would work.

Hello stalker.

"Your bike." MamaBear nodded to the car as she unlocked the front door. My mind was churning an imaginary conversation with Corbin as to the how and why he sent a text, not on retrieving my transportation.

"Sorry. Got it." I shouldered my backpack before removing the cruiser. Pushing my bike up the short, manicured sidewalk, I thanked MamaBear as she held the front door open for me. "I need to finish math before bed."

"No problem. I gotta run a load of laundry. Need clean uniforms. Need anything thrown in?"

"I think I'm good." Dirty clothes could wait until I solved the Scooby Doo mystery of who'd given Corbin my number. But I didn't want to rouse MamaBear's spidey senses, so my phone stayed in my back pocket until I closed the bathroom door.

Corbin: I think stalking is if I follow you around.

Electronic stalking. Digital age.

The water from the faucet ran until it was hot enough to wash my face. Also, it didn't sound like I was standing in the bathroom, staring at my phone.

Corbin: Good to know.

Are you going to tell me who gave you my number?

I scrubbed my mascara off then yanked a brush through my lopsided hair. My color-shifting hazel eyes were the only trait I'd inherited from my father. I used to wish I had my mom's blue eyes, but at least I inherited her perky eyebrows instead of his caterpillar unibrow.

Corbin: Zane

Had the universe imploded? I didn't remember giving Zane my

number. Maybe brushing my teeth and flossing would settle my brain while I thought of an answer.

Corbin: He had it from a youth group thing this summer. A picture hunt?

My "aha" moment popped like a bubble. It was Pastor Matt's version of a photo scavenger hunt. Adults chauffeured groups of kids around while we worked out the clues to the next point to snap group pictures. Zane's phone had run out of storage space, probably from the large amount of selfies I *happened* to see. I didn't judge—there were several shirtless ones. He'd sent the few he took of our team to me to turn in at the end of the relay. I couldn't believe he'd saved my number.

I remember now. Why didn't you ask me for it?

MamaBear knocked, and I stashed my phone to my back pocket before pulling the door open.

"You done in there?"

"Putting on my face lotion." I squirted a handful and slathered my face.

"Okay, then bed."

"Math first, then bed," I said.

I flicked off the bathroom light. My phone buzzed again. So impatient. The vibration on my behind made me scurry to the privacy of my room to figure out this guy.

MamaBear leaned forward through my door and rested her forehead against mine. "See you in the morning. Love ya."

We were exactly the same height, identical weight, even wore each other's shoes—well, I "borrowed" hers. After a bad shift, where she'd been involved with a call that hit too close to home, MamaBear would pull me into her lap. But the nights we knocked our dark brown hair lightly together was our version of a cuddle. And I liked it that way.

"Night, MamaBear."

Pajama pants are proof that God loves us and wants us to be happy. I pulled out the softest pair I had, all blue and fuzzy with cartoon manatees, and slid on a sweatshirt before even taking a glimpse at my phone. Keep him waiting.

What was I thinking? I could barely pull on my sweatshirt fast enough before my fingers were punching in the screen lock combination.

Corbin: I'm seeing the error of my ways. This is kinda creepy.
Corbin: But I didn't think of it until after you left.

A smile worked its way across my face like a tortoise.

Algebra II. Ugh. Make it go away. Maybe I'd take an easy math class my senior year. I put my phone next to the book on my bed. It only took me a few seconds to grab it back and send a reply.

Likely story. I'm sure Zane filled you in on the sordid details of my life. Like what my mom does for a living.

Although it took me a minute to realize it, I appreciated his texts. Not so much the unintended stalking issue, but his words were all spelled out. He even had punctuation!

My algebra wasn't solving its own problems, and I started down the column until the buzzing made me lose concentration. I didn't mind the break from graphing.

Corbin: Tried not to talk with him too deeply. He was more concerned with homecoming.

I snorted. That was Zane to a "T." He loved him some football, weight lifting, and his own physique. Not that his pecs made me complain.

Corbin: A mailman? No, mail lady.
Corbin: Mail person?
You're very politically correct, but no.

I continued through plotting and points while he guessed over and over. When my pencil scratched the last answer and I heaved a sigh of relief, I thumbed back over all of the incorrect answers.

Give up?
Corbin: Never give up, never surrender.

It was way past my bedtime, and my eyelids weighed down with the need to sleep. The effort to turn off the overhead light was monumental, but I made it back into bed and plugged in my phone. Alarm, check. Maybe I'd stop by for a quick visit with Marigold tomorrow.

Corbin: Waving my white flag because I'm falling asleep.

I hesitated before typing my answer. I didn't know Corbin any better than any random guy in the hallway at school. It probably wasn't the best move to give out personal information, despite the fact that he already tracked down my phone number.

To be continued...

I hoped my answer wouldn't scare him off.

———— ◦ ————

"Who's Corbin?"

Mads grabbed my phone across the lunch table as I was stealing her plastic-wrapped cupcake filled with gooey white goodness. Stupid dessert cost me my privacy.

"A guy from youth group. He came for the first time last night." Keep it simple, no details. She would lose interest and let it go. Better yet, switch and bait. "Did you pick up your dress for tomorrow?"

"Got it last night. Probably around the same time you met Corbin. Is he cute?"

"Uh, kinda?"

"Ha!" Madison popped a grape between her fire-engine-red lips. "You totally think he's cute. You're blushing. Poor Zane will be sad he's not your crush anymore."

This had to stop before she got worked up, raised her voice, and suddenly became the object of attention. It'd squash my attempt to remain relatively invisible during high school. Being a cop's kid was hard enough.

"Mads, stop. He's not hideous, but I just met him."

Her finger was busy scrolling, scrolling. She swore. "Wait. Zane has your number?"

Would my embarrassment never end? "Yeah, from a youth group thing we had over the summer. We swapped photos to participate. I didn't know he still had it." I shoved the entire cupcake into my mouth to keep from speaking.

"Color me shocked." Madison flicked off the screen and shoved my phone back across the laminate. "Please come with me tomorrow to the dance. Josh is being weird and saying he won't go." I couldn't even keep track of how many times they'd broken up and gotten back together. Their relationship was like seeing a slow-mo car wreck—horrifying and riveting at the same time.

"I can't. I'm working." Ah, yes. Corbin would see my lovely work attire. No need to spread that rumor.

Madison stuck out her lip. "Fine." It never worked on me. "You have a good time with the li'l ol' granny yesterday?"

Her question caught me off guard. I instantly hated her sarcastic, sing-song tone that usually amused me. "I'm headed there after school again."

The bell saved me. My anger flared, and I chucked my trash with a bit more force than necessary. Why in the world was I so mad about the way Mads asked about Marigold? It wasn't as if she were my grandma or anything. Still, my temper poked and prodded me all the way to American Lit.

When the final bell rang, I ignored the incessant buzzing of my phone in my pocket. I knew it was Madison, trying to apologize for making me mad. After lunch, the rest of the afternoon was a confusing push-pull of my brain trying to figure out why I was peeved about it. Really, it shouldn't have been a big deal, but every time I remembered Madison's sarcastic question, I got mad all over again. But it did help me make it to Willow Springs in record time.

Jamie nodded a recognition to me as I propped my cruiser against the wall. After I fired off a text message to MamaBear, I was on my way down the ugly, gray-flecked hallway.

"Hello." Perched on the edge of her wheelchair, a lavender-clad woman waved her skeletal hand at me. Tufts of short white hair stood on their ends over bloodshot, dark eyes.

"Hi." I gave her a dude-head-nod, jerking up my chin in acknowledgement.

"I'm Jasmine."

My feet stopped. Ugh. I was so close to Marigold's room but felt the need to be polite. "Nice to meet you. I'm on my way to see—"

"What's your name?" Her brows lifted, filling her forehead with endless wrinkles.

"Tori." I was going to be stuck in the hallway forever.

"You remind me of my goddaughter. She's beautiful too."

My heart stuttered. MamaBear called me pretty and beautiful, but she was my mom. Wasn't there a parental rule about saying nice things to their own kids?

"Thank you. I should get going now."

"Yes, okay. I'll see you soon, Tori."

When I turned the corner into Marigold's room, the air was thick and stagnant. The aroma of cleaning chemicals, stuffiness, and stale air flooded my nose. Maybe I could get a wall plug-in perfume thingy to make her room bearable.

"Victoria Grace! I didn't expect to see you today."

Resting under a thin blanket in her chair, Marigold's smile made me forget about the stench.

"I still need help finishing my homework." Really, I could've finished by myself, but now that I was here, what was the point? Besides, it was nicer listening to Marigold chat instead of being alone at the apartment.

Her bony hands patted the lace tablecloth. "Come sit down. Are you hungry? I have snacks in the cupboard next to the sink. Go ahead and take a look."

Whether I complied out of hunger or simply to be obedient,

I was shocked to find shelves filled with cupcakes, sponge cakes, individually wrapped cookies, and candy bars. Sweet manna from heaven.

"Holy moley! Jackpot!"

Marigold's giggle was adorable. She nodded when I picked two cupcakes. "I have a sweet tooth," she whispered when I handed one to her.

Suddenly famished, I polished off the snack in two bites.

"Smaller bites. You're a young woman, not an animal."

I apologized through the chocolate cake and frosting and took out my history paper.

"Now then, we left off around 1940, correct?"

"Um, yeah."

"My mistress and I were on a movie set the day Pearl Harbor was bombed in 1941. They were behind the filming schedule, and she was upset about working on a Sunday. Those poor men, they didn't even know what hit them."

Her voice faded as my pen scribbled the details: Pearl Harbor, 1941, Sunday. When my eyes popped up, Marigold gazed at the little pine tree outside her window. She seemed a million miles away.

"You always remember where you were when an important event happens." Marigold turned back to me, her eyes filled with tears. "You probably can't even remember nine-eleven."

"My mom was pregnant with me when it happened. My mom's brother worked in the second tower." My voice sounded small and distorted in my ears. I'd never known Uncle Kurt, only the stories MamaBear would rarely tell, before she shrank into silence. He seemed like he was a lot of fun to be around.

"Oh, Victoria Grace, may you never know the feeling." Marigold sniffed and adjusted her blanket, as if to reset herself. "Once the U.S. entered the war, my life was turned on end."

"I would have thought working in Hollywood had done that."

"Yes, well, it was nothing compared to war." She explained food and clothing rations, along with scrap metal drives.

"Since I knew how to write letters, I would take the bus down to Glendale and help out the pilots with their letters home. Sometimes, it was for the mechanics and other men working on the base. I'd write out a nice letter, and they would sign it." She cocked her head to the side and smiled. "It's always nice to receive a letter in the mail. Phones were hard to come by back then."

I pushed back in my chair. "I check in with MamaBear every few hours."

"They were lucky to send home letters every week or so." Marigold nibbled at her cupcake. "That's where I met my husband."

"Aw!" I loved sneaking in to watch the end of romantic movies. I could already imagine the girl from the silver-framed pictured coyly writing a letter for the handsome soldier in his uniform. "How long were you married?"

She hummed and looked back outside. Had I stuck my foot in my mouth with the question?

"Maybe we'll get to him another time. But you have homework, Victoria Grace, and I will not be swayed with a story. Onward and upward."

For the next two hours, I wrote details from her immaculate memory. Marigold spoke with her hands, gnarled and waving in excitement, folded and still in sorrow as she remembered entire Japanese families disappearing on overcrowded buses.

My stomach rumbled in hunger when an employee delivered her covered dinner tray.

"Would you like to share?" she asked.

Scared that there would be some type of turkey-gravy and gross instant mashed potatoes under the blue lid, I declined and slipped my backpack over my shoulders.

My nagging inner snoop fought with common sense until I caved into my curiosity. A sly peek confirmed that there was no wedding ring on Marigold's hand as she uncovered her meal.

Maybe it was too hard to push on past her contorted knuckles, or maybe it was stored in her sock drawer.

Good thing that I needed more community service hours to figure it out.

Seven

CANNED RAVIOLIS WERE MY SPECIALTY. I DUMPED A can into a bowl and shoved it into the microwave. Scrolling through Instagram, I waited for my gourmet dinner to warm when my cell phone chirped.

Corbin: Is it weird to admit that I'm nervous about tomorrow?

I grabbed my food out and sat at the counter before I answered. He was still waiting for a response on MamaBear's job.

It's weird to admit to someone you met yesterday.

If he could get past my sarcasm, we could be friends. But then again, he did watch Shelby's rear end. Testosterone was a gigantic mystery I didn't have time for. Car, scholarship, get out of Redding. College would have more male options.

Corbin: Feels like I've known you longer.

I blew on a forkful of ravioli, trying to figure out if his response was creepy.

Corbin: That was creepy.

Corbin: I'll shut up now.

His text made me grunt. How did we think the same exact thing? It seemed like a good time to drop the bomb and see if he would flee altogether.

Kinda creepy. Careful, or my mom will arrest you for harassment.

My phone remained dark and silent while I polished off my

dinner. How disappointing. He actually seemed like someone fun to hang out with at youth group or see in the hallways.

I ran a load of laundry and set out my clothes for the following day. My favorite black shirt declared "I love you" in block white letters, with the last word crossed out and replaced with "tacos." It made me smile every time I wore it.

When I rolled my work pants and shirt into my backpack, I double-checked my phone. Still *nada*. I prepared myself for awkward chitchat at the theater the next night.

The phone growled when I was in the middle of scrubbing my forehead.

MamaBear: Bedtime.

I know. Washing my face.

MamaBear: How was Marigold today?

She used to write letters for soldiers in WW2. Her room smells like a troll cave.

I scrunched my nose thinking about the distinct aroma.

Can you pick up a plug in or candle?

MamaBear: Not sure a candle is the best option in a place with dementia patients.

Good call. Don't want anyone to burn it down when they remember their pyromania tendencies.

MamaBear: I'll think about it. Go to bed, spawn. Love you.

Love you too. Night.

I made sure the alarm was set, turned the phone to vibrate, and wiggled against my blanket until I was comfortable. Deep in thought about Marigold's secret husband and her letter writing, I let my mind roam. Was he a pilot or part of the grounds crew? Wait! Maybe he was a spy and they wrote their letters in code.

Under my blanket, my phone buzzed.

Corbin: Sorry. No cell phones at dinner with Grammy. Or dessert. And then poker.

I rubbed my eyes. Yup. I read that correctly.

Poker with Grammy...

Corbin: We play for money and she won $50.

Not being a professional or even amateur card player, I winged my response.

Grammy is a hustler.

Corbin: At least she gave me another slice of pie before she took my money.

If I had fifty extra bucks, it would be in my bank account, not on a poker table. But then again, I didn't have any grandparents. Maybe poker was their Thursday night tradition.

Don't tell me. Homemade apple pie?

Corbin: Store bought chocolate cream.

I liked Grammy more and more. She made pies exactly the same way I did.

What time is your grand tour?

Sweet mother, I was tired. The deeper my exhaustion, the more my nose itched, and it felt like a bug was crawling in my nostrils. Ew.

Corbin: 9

I'm falling asleep. Let me know how it goes and what your schedule is. Maybe we'll have a class together.

After I sent the text, my brain mocked its desperate tone. Why would I care if we had a class together? I hoped he'd translate it as me being overly friendly. I could only wish.

Corbin: Night

Excellent. Wait, not excellent. Now I had to be friendly.

———¬ ◦ |———

MamaBear must've had a rough shift because she packed my lunch and left it on the counter the next morning. She only did that when she needed to not think about something that happened during the night, to think about me before she fell asleep. That was how she explained it once. I added it to my backpack and headed to school in the drizzling rain. Why couldn't it be overcast? Or stupid hot? At least my hooded jacket kept my hair from giving me the appearance of a drowned rat on the ride.

Madison greeted me at the bike rack, holding her umbrella over me while I chained up my bike. "You sure you don't want to come tonight? Pleeeeease?"

"Josh still being a jerkface?"

"Pretty much. I think he'll come, but he won't say so."

"Still have to work." I sidestepped a puddle on the sidewalk as the first bell rang. Oh no.

I darted down the hall and called back to Madison, whose dad really never kept track of the twenty or more tardies she racked up. "Sorry, Mads. Gotta go. Can't be late."

My dripping jacket made tiny pools around my seat. My mind was far away, bouncing between figuring out who would be working at the theater that night and if I'd run into Corbin during his tour—not that I wanted or needed to see him. I fought to concentrate on the progressive tenses of the Spanish verbs, instead of wondering if anyone would see Corbin's leg and automatically categorize him into the pyramid scheme of high school life.

In U.S. History, Mr. Hammond collected the essays. I held my breath on his approach, to try to inhale the least amount of his sour body odor. When he grabbed my three-page report, his bushy eyebrows tweaked. "Seems a bit lengthy for a 500-word assignment."

Thirty-two heads swiveled toward me. I wanted to crawl under my desk.

"I found it interesting and got a bit carried away." At least I didn't lie.

Mr. Hammond breathed out a "humph" before he moved down the row. All of the eyes in the room turned away and resumed their frantic scribbling or covert cell phone usage. Who actually thinks they can stare at their belly button and look normal?

Creative Writing issued a thousand-word story due on Monday, any topic. The catch? Exactly 1,000 words. No problem for me. I shoveled out anonymous stories on fan fiction sites all the time.

At lunch, I took out my phone. Nothing from Corbin or MamaBear. Great. Was he going to pop up in the cafeteria? I slid into an empty spot at a table to wait for Madison.

Corbin: I'm going to get lost.

I knew how he felt. In my first week at Butte as a sophomore, I got turned around more than a few times. Merciful teachers saw my panicked face and pointed me across the hallway or to another building.

Print out a map. That's what I had to do.

Corbin: Got one from Miss Peach.

Could a guidance counselor have a more ridiculous name?

What's your schedule?

Madison landed with a dramatic sigh across the table.

I stashed my phone into my pocket to avoid her need-to-know basis of my life. This "thing" with Corbin was new, and I wanted it for myself for now. Her nosiness knew no bounds or social media editing.

"I'll pay you to go to homecoming. Call in sick."

However tempting, I declined. Faced with sweeping popcorn from theater floors or being the third wheel in the Madison-Josh saga, I chose my neon green work shirt. Less drama.

"You've never been to a dance! This is high school, Tori. You're supposed to go to football games, parties, and dances."

I had zero interest in the activities Madison listed. She was the closest thing I had to a best friend. Often, I wondered what we even had in common, besides a random love of *Dr. Who*. And she didn't even watch any of the new episodes.

"I have to work. My dad didn't give me a car." My hasty words stung my own ears.

Madison's eyebrows dropped. She swiped her lunch pail and scrambled up. I could only stand and see her speed away, feeling like an idiot.

I did the only thing I could do.

Mads, I'm sorry. It came out all wrong, but I still am sorry.

And her answer told me exactly where I could go.

My appetite vanished. I fled to my locker, carefully surveying the hallway to make sure she wasn't bawling at the neighboring door. This day was going down the toilet fast.

"Hey."

I yanked my head from behind my open locker, and Corbin grinned at me. At his elbow, an older woman with long white hair smiled at me. She looked straight out of a vintage Betty Crocker ad, Texas style: luxurious waves past her shoulders, a crisp, baby blue shirt with matching buttons, rounded out with blue jeans and well-worn roper boots.

"You must be Grammy." I shoved my hand forward, like MamaBear taught me many years ago.

Her grip made me clench my teeth. "Guilty as charged. And you would be Tori."

"Yup. Though we should let him make the introductions so he feels included." I tilted my head toward Corbin, who was still smiling like a dork with the latest director's cut of *Star Wars*.

"Oh, don't mind me. I'm only here for moral support." He twisted to glance down the hall. "That and I still have no idea which way to go."

"I'll show you to the front. Hopefully you can find your way to your car." I shouldered my backpack and walked on the opposite side of Grammy. "How does your schedule look?"

Grammy chuckled. "Poor boy has to retake a couple of history classes. Seems the state of California doesn't like that Texas allowed him to pass World History with only five credits and he'll need to retake it to graduate here."

"That's rude, especially if he passed," I said.

Corbin scoffed. "I passed."

"Well, it's all a bunch of nonsense to me. He got all As back at

Liberty Hill." Grammy paused at the double doors while Corbin pushed them open. "Thank you, Corbie."

I mouthed her pet name for him when I passed, and he made a face while shaking his head. The bell interrupted any further childish pranks.

"I gotta get to American Lit, but send me a text with your schedule. I'll help you map it out over the weekend."

He bobbed his chin and offered his elbow to Grammy. It was cute watching them chat arm in arm as they headed to the parking lot.

Wouldn't you know it? He helped her into passenger side of a 1970 faded midnight-blue Mustang with Texas plates parked in the visitor's spot.

Eight

SWEET, SWEET FREEDOM CAME AT TWO-THIRTY FRIDAY afternoon. I'd already rounded up my homework into my backpack so I didn't have a weird moment at the lockers with Madison. She was angry. I was sorry. But she also didn't care to hear my apology. I got it—I'd been there. It would work itself out, eventually.

Purple and white football jerseys crammed the hallways. Butte Bulldog sweatshirts disappeared under jackets as I dodged my way out to the bike rack. My shift started in an hour, and I needed every spare minute to grab a bite to eat, change, and brush my teeth to combat nacho breath the entire shift.

Is it crazy that the local taco shop knew me by my order? Right down to the extra olives, please.

Big, fat raindrops pelted the windows of the restaurant as I crunched my way through dinner. I pulled my phone out of my back pocket. Better send MamaBear a text before I clocked in. Besides, there were times she couldn't get back to me for hours on a busy Friday night. Criminals didn't care if she needed a bathroom break.

Nachos almost tasted homemade. Headed to work. Be safe.

Although it was homecoming at Butte, the other local high schools had seemingly dumped into the theater by the time I pushed my bike to the employee break room. If it was this packed already, it'd be nuts later. The people who liked to say that a busy shift passed quickly had never swept stale popcorn and mopped dumped sodas for hours at a time.

After shrugging on my safety-green shirt, I used the bathroom mirror to line my eyes with heavy black eyeliner. I had to grind out every Friday night with a broom, hoping no one would recognize me. My friend wasn't talking to me. I was invisible to any guy who was remotely cute. My eyes needed to be as black as my mood.

Somewhere between the six o'clock rush and the nine PM crowd, I was pushing the mini vacuum near the exits farthest from the podium. How people managed to spill this much popcorn this far away from trashcans was beyond me, but I volunteered. It put me beyond Mr. Bolt's beady eyes shifting between my nail polish and my permanent marker doodles, as if I were Satan himself.

I sang along with a soundtrack playing in the hallway speakers, enjoying my tiny slice of freedom.

"And she sings too."

I jumped sideways with a squeak, and the vacuum handle banged into the wall. My coworkers loved to scare me since I was a tad on the jumpy side, but this voice had a distinct drawl.

I retrieved the vacuum and turned it off before turning and lifting my chin. "Hey."

Corbin pushed up the bill of his ballcap. "Had no idea you worked here."

"Not something I advertise." I smoothed my shirt. "I mean, I probably should, with this spectacular uniform."

He tilted his head one way and then the other. "I suppose, in a construction worker way."

"What're you watching?" I scanned the hall to see if Mr. Bolt was stalking me. All clear.

"Grammy wanted to see this one." He nodded to the door near the vacuum's cord.

"Never pegged you for a rodeo movie type of guy, being from Texas."

"It's crazy. I even won a buckle for mutton busting once."

"For what busting?"

"Mutton busting. I rode on a sheep when I was five." Corbin clearly was enjoying my lack of knowledge on the subject and grinned widely.

From the corner of my eye, someone in an equally fluorescent green shirt moved in the hallway, and I flicked on the power to the vacuum again. "Gotta get back to work or my boss will fly down on his broom."

"All right, see ya."

I tried not to outright stare as he sauntered toward the bathroom. Instead, I conveniently positioned myself to have to glance up in his general direction as I was cleaning the carpet. Neither spy nor ninja, I half-heartedly waved as he went back into the auditorium.

I didn't dare look at my phone until my break rolled around. More than one poor soul was fired when Mr. Bolt caught them checking a text, and I was too close to my half of the car payment to mess that up.

MamaBear: Fridays are always such fun. Good times with drunks before 6 p.m.

As I was typing my response, Madison sent me a selfie from the bathroom in the gym at school. Her perfect blonde curls framed her downturned lips.

Mads: You should be here.

And just like that, our disagreement was behind us. It was how we worked. I stepped into the employee bathroom and returned a selfie, making sure my repulsive top took up half of the frame.

Couldn't pass up this shirt. It compliments my skin tone.

Mads: At least Josh showed up.

Slow dancing would've been awkward with three of us.

She filled my screen with laughing emojis and gifs.

I figured she returned to the dance, and I switched back to my mom.

Become a cop, they said. It'll be fun, they said.

While MamaBear didn't discourage me from becoming an officer, she didn't urge me to run to the badge, even though I still contemplated law enforcement—maybe forensics. I'd made up my mind to skip being a street cop when I was fifteen, on the morning I woke up and she was curled around me, still in her uniform. A teenage girl wrapped her car around a tree after drinking at a party, and MamaBear was first on the scene. I could still see where the tears had run down MamaBear's cheeks as she softly snored into my pillow.

MamaBear: Off at 2?

Hopefully 1:30. I'll let you know.

MamaBear: See ya then.

I'd finished reading my mom's text when Corbin's buzzed through.

Corbin: It was a good movie.

Although I wanted to get into a lengthy conversation about riding sheep, my break was over. I plodded back downstairs and moved from one messy theater to another, endlessly sweeping and emptying trash cans.

My hair smelled like stale popcorn when I crawled into MamaBear's car after my shift ended. I only knew I needed a shower and sleep. But mostly sleep.

———◦———

No idea how I stayed upright during my shower when I got home, but suddenly I was waking up in my bed the next morning. The sunshine found my eyes no matter which way I twisted. Frustrated and hungry, I moped to the kitchen. My shift didn't start until five and the Branches hadn't called, so I was free to lounge and check out the pictures Mads had sent to me. I flipped on the TV to see if there were any cartoons or Bob Ross reruns. Happy little trees made my Saturday mornings bearable.

I planned on following through with lying around in my

pajamas until a cute commercial with old people came on and made me think of Marigold. She probably was sitting in her room all alone. And that was sad.

Besides, it was for school credits. And it was all about dazzling those scholarship committees.

My laziness lost out. I pulled an oversized sweatshirt I'd bought on a vacation to the Oregon coast over my favorite pair of jeans. Popped off a text to MamaBear, laced up my Chucks, and I was on my way to Willow Springs. Maybe a short visit, an hour tops, to make her happy, and then I'd go home until I had to leave for work.

"What a pleasant surprise!" Marigold motioned for me to sit at the empty chair across the table from her. "Come for another visit, have you?"

"Well, I have a little time and thought I'd come say hi before I have to go to work."

"Yes, yes. Earning money for your car. Very industrious of you, Victoria Grace."

"Let me take a picture of us together so MamaBear believes me." I crouched next to her chair and into the camera frame with her. We leaned our heads together—a contrast of brown hair to white, smooth freckled skin beside years of wrinkles, my hazel eyes next to her sky blue ones.

I sat back down in my chair. "It's either work or don't have a car. The choice is pretty cut-and-dry for me."

A buzz interrupted our talk, and I checked my phone.

Nicky: Hey Squirt

My cousin would probably punch my arm and leave the biggest bruise if he saw his childhood nickname programmed into my phone. I didn't care if he was twenty-one and in the army. He was the closest thing I had to a brother growing up.

Hi! Long time, no talk! I don't have any money you can borrow.

Nicky: don't have long but I needed to tell u b4 u hear. Shipping to Afghanistan.

Invisible fingers wound their way around my heart and squeezed as I reread his text. He was only a mechanic. He wasn't supposed to be deployed.

When?

It probably was only thirty seconds for his reply, but the silence stretched. I felt Marigold's eyes on me from across the table but didn't dare look up.

Nicky: 2 weeks top

Who was the moron that made the decision to send him? He was Uncle Kent's sole child and my only cousin. My heart skittered and I blinked through the onslaught of tears. Nick needed me to be strong. He wanted me to tell him it would be okay, like the time his dog Tink died and I held his hand when we buried her in his mom's backyard.

But I suddenly had no idea what to say. An apology was weak. It was too raw to type back about getting a sunburn or getting sand everywhere. My thumb hovered over the keys.

"Are you all right, Victoria Grace?"

Marigold's soft voice broke my inner raging storm. It wasn't fair they were sending him.

"My cousin is being deployed to Afghanistan," I said. You know those times when your own voice sounds far away? It felt like my brain was running out the door, while my body gave up in the rigid folding chair.

"Oh, child, that is a hard one." She reached across the table and patted my hand, making my screen jiggle. "You two are close?"

"He's like my brother." I was surprised to hear my voice catch in my throat. The only time Nick made me cry was when he dropped me a few years before and split my lip.

My phone lit up again.

Nicky: u there???

"I don't know what to say to him," I whispered.

Gnarled fingers latched onto my wrist. "Tell him you love him and to be safe. Every man needs to hear that from his family."

I knew she was right, but it sounded cliché and hollow.

I'm proud of you. Love you and send me info when you can.

Nicky: luv u 2 squirt. Tell ur mom? I couldn't care less if every word was misspelled, abbreviated, or not capitalized.

Yup. Be safe.

For a few moments, or maybe it was longer, I stared at my phone. He was across the country, so it wasn't like I could bike over to his base. Regrets bombed my brain: if I'd only gone to the barbeque last time Nick was visiting, instead of being embarrassed that his high school buddies would be there. Or tried to send him a card or two while he was at Fort Stewart.

"When World War II sent boys overseas by the shipful, there were lots of women left at home." Marigold pulled back her hand and dropped it into her lap. "My mistress and I helped how we could, mostly in the Hollywood Canteen. But when the telegram arrived, telling me my brother had been killed, I had to do more."

Marigold's eyes sparkled with unshed tears. She sniffed into her handkerchief. "Harold was only a year older than me. I didn't even get to see him in his uniform. Only a few weeks later, my own telegram came to my mistress' house, informing me of the Naval Department's deepest regrets for my husband."

I held my breath. Maybe I'd get bits about her husband, since she blew me off last time.

"It wasn't like I knew Kenneth at all. We were married less than a month before he shipped out. I was happy when he left. The man he was at home was not the same pilot on base, in front of friends and commanders."

She paused, looking out the window. Not the same man? Did he…hurt her? I clenched my fists.

"If anything," she continued, "the telegram made me miss my brother more. Besides, the Navy couldn't return Kenneth's body." She scrutinized the atrium, her voice factual and clipped. "It was

Harold I had in mind when I took the bus to the Pasadena Area Station Hospital. Those boys, the same age as my brother, missing bits and pieces—it was my duty to write letters home for them or to their pals still fighting."

I conjured up a young Marigold, sitting on a metal chair between hospital beds, furiously scribbling down a letter before she interrupted my daydream.

"It was inhumane." Her voice wavered. "There was no air conditioning. Doctors were few and nurses spread thin. Between my mistress and the Canteen, I could only go a few times a week, and every time, the smell made me retch."

"That sounds awful."

Her cheeks were rosy. "I had no choice. I saw Harold in every face."

I glanced back at my phone, the screen now dark. "I can email him while he's over there."

Marigold clucked her tongue and I looked up. One of her white eyebrows arched high. "It is special holding a letter and reading the slant of the writing that is far more personable than an email."

"But he can read it quicker and I can attach pictures."

"He cannot fold it into a pocket and take it out when he needs it most."

"He's my cousin…I'm not going to put perfume on it." Um, gross.

Her heavy lids narrowed. "Your cousin deserves more than a cursory, half-thought out, rushed email, Victoria Grace."

Marigold's accusation slapped my excuses with a satisfying smack. I was a jerk for trying to shortchange my cousin.

I blew my breath out through my lips and closed my eyes. Her warm hand once again surrounded mine.

"Child…Tori." Her face softened by the time my eyes fluttered open. "Give him a gift—the gift of your time."

Ugh. She was right. I nodded.

And my brain was suddenly in overdrive with the thought.

"What if I wrote to him *and* the guys in his unit? Like random letters for him to pass out?"

A sincere smile lit up her aged face. "What a lovely idea! If you would like, I could help you. I don't have anything scheduled between bingo and physical therapy."

I flung from search engine to sites on my phone, searching for ideas. There had to be a company or group who could help us get started.

Boom! Found it.

I swiveled the tiny screen to face Marigold, then kneeled on the linoleum next to her elbow. "How does this look?"

"It's too small for me to read. You read it to me."

I read the statement for the volunteer organization. She hummed in agreement.

My phone alarm pinged. It was four-thirty in the afternoon?

For the first time ever, I was going to be late to work.

Nine

AN HOUR LATER, AFTER I'D GRITTED MY TEETH WHILE being lectured on the privilege of working at such a "fine theater" and then shuffling between theater auditoriums with coworkers who couldn't let go of the fact I had been an entire fifteen minutes late, I was on my hands and knees on the purple-and-black carpet. Though he didn't *say* it was punishment, Mr. Bolt handed me a bottle of cleaning solution, a scraper, and gloves and put me on the humiliating task of removing gum and anything else stuck in the carpet pile. The blue gloves added a sense of elegance as I scooched my way down the long hall.

"Fancy meeting you here," said a drawled voice nearby.

Really? He came to the movies two nights in a row?

"I'd greet you properly, but my gloves are really necessary for this lovely task." My neck hurt when I tipped my head nearly vertical.

"It looks super important."

I worked the scraper under a crusty piece of fossilized food. "Yeah, well, my boss is a sadist and a bit of a power freak." It finally popped free and I spied another nearby. "I was late to work and he wanted to remind me not to do it again."

Corbin's metal ankle creaked when he crouched down next to me. "Tardiness will not be tolerated."

"Pretty much." My foot tingled from being trapped in a strange angle. "What are you here to see?"

He pulled a ticket stub from the back pocket of his jeans. "Uh, this one?"

"It's decent. I've sat in on a few breaks." I gathered my supplies, glancing to see if Mr. Bolt was spying around the corner, and stood. "Oh, my legs hurt so bad."

Corbin hoisted himself up and shook the pant leg over the slip of metal at his ankle. He noticed me watching. "I keep it covered in public because the girls all want to touch it and it makes me blush."

Was he for real? I looked up and he grinned.

"You should make business cards to hand out," I countered.

"I would, but it would be cliché."

My eyebrows climbed. If he wanted to tango, I was his Huckleberry. "An ace in the hole."

"It's nothing to sneeze at."

"Sounds right up your alley."

"You can't fit a square peg in a round hole," he said. And there was that dimple.

"You snooze, you lose."

"Goin' out in a blaze of glory." Texans didn't need the "g" ending.

"Cry me a river, bub."

His laughter bounced off the hallway walls. "You can't go throw Wolverine into this. That's cheating."

I smirked. "Deal with it."

"Tori!" Mr. Bolt's nasal call pulled me out of my happy place. Anywhere was better than crawling on the carpet.

I moved to another area and sat down. "He's going to blow an artery and put me in concessions if I don't finish before the nine o'clock shows." My hands were sweating inside the rubber gloves.

"All right. I'll see you tomorrow." He gave me a dude-head-nod, then disappeared behind the door. I looked up just in time to see him glance back at me.

My scraper jammed against faintly minty, yet petrified gum. Yum.

Oh wait. Corbin said he'd see me the next day. Sunday. At church. I mentally catalogued my wardrobe and then stopped.

Why did I care? I'd only met the guy, what, a few days ago. Weirdo, creepy stalker who sat in my chair and showed up at my work.

But he did have a Mustang.

I would wear a skirt. No, pants—but not jeans. But if jeans were my only clean pants, they wouldn't have holes.

———⌐ ₀ ⌐———

"You're fancy this morning." MamaBear worked a shift trade with another officer and had a free Sunday. She pushed a cup of coffee to me.

I took a sip. Perfect amount of creamer. "Thanks."

No, I would not take the bait and talk about the skirt around my waist. I'd bought it on a whim at a thrift store over the summer because the cream-colored lace was pretty and not too girly and the length didn't make me feel like a hooker, like some of the girls at school. Harsh, but it was the truth.

"That shirt looks good on you."

Hopefully there was an English muffin. I moved toward the toaster, slyly eyeing at my top. Black, of course, since it was my favorite color, with the tiniest cream-colored pin stripes. The long sleeves were rolled to my elbows.

"Do you want to borrow my black flats?" she asked.

"Mom, stop!"

She would keep quizzing me until I broke. Trio meowed near the cupboard, asking for more food in her half-full bowl.

"What? I only said you looked nice."

"It's what you're *not* saying." I pushed the English muffin into the toaster before I spun to face her. MamaBear's innocent face didn't impress me. "I'm wearing my Converse and I felt like wearing a skirt."

MamaBear made her hands into claws and hissed at me. "Back down, tiger. Drink your coffee and let the caffeine flow through your veins. We're leaving in fifteen minutes."

I ducked into the bathroom to reassess my hair and makeup. Hairspray kept the tiny hairs in place above my left ear. It showcased my favorite ear cuff, chained to my earring. Perfect black eyeliner with a bit of cat eye. Hopefully someone, anyone, besides my mom would appreciate it, even if it was Bob, the chatty old usher with his white wiry beard. I glanced at the seldom used bottle of perfume and decided against it. MamaBear would go full-on detective with a faint whiff of vanilla.

The least I could do was clean the scuff marks off of my low tops to dress them up. I contemplated accepting MamaBear's black flats, but then she would win and that wouldn't do first thing on a Sunday morning. She was already circling the bathroom door like a shark, smelling something different. And it wasn't my deodorant.

We sat in the same spot we always did when we went to church together: left side of the sanctuary, third row from the back, aisle seat and the one next to it. I never asked to sit on the aisle seat because I never argued with MamaBear's police explanations. There were certain rules I had: always answer a text, never answer the door, and don't ask to sit on the aisle seat.

Sitting on the inside had its advantages. Usually no one tried to squeeze by to sit in the empty three chairs next to us. But it also meant I didn't have full view of the room to, say, try and find a certain person. Like the lanky Texan in plaid, who cruised up the opposite side of the sanctuary by the time I could sneak a peek, when MamaBear grabbed her lip balm from her purse. It's not like I wanted him to sit by me, though. Try explaining that to Investigator Weston. No thanks.

Okay, I was a bit unsocial during the painfully awkward time where you're supposed to turn around and greet your neighbor. Personally, I think it's plain weird.

"Hi, stranger. Say your name. I'll smile and pretend I'll remember, but I see you staring at my nose ring."

Not my idea of a good time. I'd rather hunker down in my armchair on Wednesday nights and brood. And for that very reason, I refused to glance across the sea of hair, even though I was sure Corbin waited for me to look his way. Instead, I forced myself to say hello to the lady behind us, her baby swaddled tight in a sling across her chest. Jennie? No...Jenae. Or maybe it was Janice.

Later, as the sermon wound down, I crammed my bulletin into my pocket. I'd been doodling the entire time, trying to envision the least amount of interaction with Corbin and MamaBear. The longer she was with him, the more questions she'd ask. It brought her great joy to see me squirm. And in front of a guy? I was kinda terrified for church to dismiss.

She maneuvered a path out of the sanctuary. "Wanna go get lunch and then look for jeans?"

"I need jeans."

"Yes, that's why I offered. You keep reminding me." She made a face at me and I tried to peep over her shoulder. I should've known better because she's a trained observer. "Who's back there?" MamaBear twisted about the same time Grammy and Corbin were a few feet away.

"Hey." I nodded to him. "Hi, Grammy."

Something magical happened. Before MamaBear even uttered a humiliating word, Corbin shot out his hand. "Hello, ma'am." God bless his accent. It made his introduction even better since she liked Westerns. "Corbin Dallas. This is my Grammy, Rosabelle Dallas."

Rosabelle? How absolutely adorable! With a name like that, I almost imagined her in a pink off-the-shoulder, frilly, hoop-skirted dress as a young girl.

Grammy extended her hand. "Hello."

"Kacey Weston. Nice to meet you both." Though her words were perfectly normal, her suspicious tone was directed at me. She thought I was keeping a boy hidden from her.

"Corbin was at youth group on Wednesday and starts at Butte tomorrow," I said, to jog her memory.

"Yeah, I was going to show Tori my schedule." He pulled a folded paper from the pocket of his flannel. "Wanted to see if we had any of the same classes in case I get lost."

I jumped in before MamaBear could start. "I saw him on Friday when he registered and had to show him the way to the parking lot." Oh please, oh please, don't let her play ninety questions.

"Would you like to come to lunch with us?" she asked the pair.

That was unexpected from Señora Snoopy. I could remember exactly how many times she invited strangers to eat with us: zero.

"Why, yes, sweetheart." Grammy's smile revealed a row of uneven teeth. "That would be super. We'll have to follow you 'cause we don't know our way around yet."

"No problem." MamaBear was suddenly in control of the conversation. This could go very poorly for me.

Grammy walked next to MamaBear through the foyer and into the parking lot. Corbin and I developed a case of lag, falling farther behind.

"Let's see the damage, Corbie." I unfolded his schedule.

"It's irritatin' starting the day off with two history classes."

"Blech. At least World History is a freshman class. Think of all the fun you'll have crammed into a class of noobs." I glanced further down the page. "Oh, hey! I get to see your bright, shiny face in second period. Mr. Hammond is a bore, but he teaches straight from the book so it's easy."

"You two coming?" MamaBear squinted at me.

Go away, Mom. "Yep."

She didn't say a word when I slid into the passenger seat beside her. I flipped through my phone, ignoring her sideways glare. They weren't subtle. I could almost feel her silent questions all the way to lunch.

The Black Bear Diner was my favorite place to eat. It was where MamaBear took me when we moved to Redding, and the day I'd received a random birthday card from my father after six years of nothing. I pushed the five dollar bill into the offering at church and inhaled a small chocolate cream pie later in the day.

I already knew what I wanted: the two-egg breakfast special with hash browns and a vanilla shake. Breakfast was the only meal I could eat at any time of the day.

My order appeared dainty compared to the mountain o' food Corbin gobbled down. He stayed relatively quiet while MamaBear and Grammy politely sorted details. I was mid-bite when my phone buzzed in my lap.

Corbin: This is going well. Thought your mom would read me my rights by now.

That's next week.

Corbin: I know what's coming. I planned on telling you later.

I eyeballed him across the table. The corner of Corbin's mouth tucked sideways. His sad eyes dropped to the stack of pancakes.

"After Corbin's accident, he came to live with us." Grammy took a quick swig of water before continuing. "I mean, after he was released from the hospital."

MamaBear's face was passive, but I saw a bunch of replies in her still eyes. She swung into "cop mode," her voice even and steady. "I didn't know he was hospitalized." Her foot tapped against mine under the table. Like I had time to explain he had a prosthetic leg.

Grammy hummed and patted Corbin's hand. He kept examining his fork, layering bacon, pancakes, and potatoes.

"When he was twelve, his family was in a terrible car accident." Grammy's voice quivered. "My son, his wife, and Corbin's little sister were killed by a girl who was driving and texting. It was a miracle Corbie survived at all."

Geez.

I wanted to say I was sorry, wanted to apologize for anything offensive I may have said. Instead, I studied my eggs and didn't feel like eating at all.

"He was a trouper, with all of the physical therapy and fittings and learning to adapt." From the corner of my eye, Grammy's thumb rubbed tiny circles on her index finger.

"I can only imagine." MamaBear's voice dropped its methodic, professional edge.

I shoveled food into my mouth to stay busy and fired off a text with my other hand.

Would it be weird to say I'm sorry?

"When Papa, my husband, passed last year, his sister needed a little extra help." Grammy cleared her throat and straightened in her chair. "Besides, a change of scenery was good for us. My other son, Richard, has the ranch in hand."

Corbin: Nah. Everyone says that.

"Do you have any classes together?" Suddenly, I was back in MamaBear's crosshairs.

"Yeah, second period, U.S. History." I wasn't about to fess up to the shared lunch period.

Grammy jabbed Corbin with her elbow. "At least you'll know somebody."

"We have American Lit and Chemistry, but not at the same time." For the first time since the meal started, Corbin spoke. "Same teachers, too." Sneaky boy, not spilling the beans about lunch. He was onto MamaBear and her factfinding ways.

I was stuck. Part of me wanted to ask questions about his family, and the other part of me told myself to shut up and not be a jerk.

"How long have you had your car?" I asked. Figured a question like that couldn't hurt.

Corbin's fork paused on its way to his mouth. "Um, it was my dad's."

And there it was—Victoria Grace, the jerkface.

"Well, honey," Grammy reached over and patted my hand,

"Papa bought it new for him brand, spankin' new from the lot. There's a picture of it back at the ranch."

Oh! I could make it out of the hole I was in with the right question. "What's the name of your ranch?"

"Hollow Heart."

Perfect. I was paving my personal highway to hell.

Ten

ALTHOUGH GRAMMY TRIED TO CONSOLE ME WITH THE fact that her great-great grandpappy named the ranch after a heart-shaped hollow in the crook of a tree, it didn't make me feel any better. I knew if I opened my mouth again, I'd somehow pull Corbin's sister or mother's name out of the clear blue sky. I focused on my milkshake.

Corbin: You look like you accidentally kicked a puppy.

Anything I sent would sound horrible or stupid, so I powered down my phone. Really, I didn't need to be a bigger idiot.

"You want me to drop you off at Marigold's?" MamaBear's question pulled me out of my funk.

"Uh, hadn't even thought about it, but that'd be fine." What happened to shopping for jeans?

"Marigold's." Grammy slipped cash into the folder the waiter dropped off. "That sounds like a fancy tea shop."

MamaBear leveled her eyes at me. I didn't want to explain. If I said it was for the youth group assignment, it would sound shallow. And school credits? Then it would strengthen the heartless teenager comments from a few minutes ago. Instead, I crammed my straw into my mouth, thinking the question would die in silence.

Wrong.

"Tori volunteers at a care facility near our apartment." Gee, thanks, Mom.

Even as I busied myself with my napkin, I could see Grammy's wide smile. "How wonderful!"

I remembered my manners and muttered, "Thank you."

"What made you decide to volunteer, Tori?"

I prayed for a hole to swallow me. Or maybe I'd have a heart attack. "It was for a youth group project." Better to be lame than callous.

Across from me, Corbin not-so-casually stretched under the table, knocking his legs against mine. When I looked up, he wiggled his phone at me. I quickly shook my head and stood up, since Grammy rose, dropping her napkin onto her empty plate. Run away. Flee the scene. Work up the courage to send a text later.

"Wait up!" Corbin's shoes slapped the sidewalk beside me after I pushed out of the diner. "You okay?"

"Sorry about your family and the ranch name. I had no idea."

"I know." He walked beside me even when I sped up toward the car.

"I…I'm sorry I brought it up."

His hand caught my elbow. "It's okay. You didn't know. I don't tell many people." Corbin shifted his chin forward and sniffed. "People get all weird and mopey and apologize over and over."

"I only apologized twice."

One side of his mouth slanted up. "You have that going for you."

"You ready, Tori?" MamaBear clicked the door locks.

"Yup." I waved to Corbin and Grammy before dropping into the passenger seat and shutting the door. "Don't say anything," I pled. I turned my phone on to avoid seeing her.

From the corner of my eye, I could see MamaBear's smile as she turned the key in the ignition. I knew that grin. That was the "he's-a-cute-boy" face. After the smile, she'd string out questions to figure out if I liked him as a friend or as a boy she would have to put through the ringer.

"Pretty tragic about his family." MamaBear dealt with enough collisions and informing family members to know how to phrase the horrible situation.

"Yeah." What else could I say? The only way to divert her was a topic change. "Will you pick me up later?"

"Sure. You said you wanted to finish up your Algebra homework? Are you going to do that with Marigold?"

"Might as well. My books and laptop are in the back."

Her knuckles tightened around the steering wheel. "You left your stuff in the car? Tori."

"I know, I'm sorry." Thank goodness Willow Springs was around the corner.

She didn't say another word. It frightened me when she was silent, stewing, and planning my impending doom for leaving my laptop where it could have been stolen.

MamaBear stopped the car at the curb. "I'll be back around six."

"Thank you." I batted my eyelashes.

She tried to glare but smiled. "Love you, kid. Get your stuff and the diffuser thingy I bought. I gotta hot date with the DVR."

"Nice. Don't forget to catch up on that new show. I already watched the first five episodes." I slammed the door shut and grinned through the window. MamaBear laughed, shaking her head as she drove away.

I jerked my head up to acknowledge the weekend lady at the front counter. As the days passed, I was able to find my own way to Marigold's room without backtracking or asking for directions. Residents knew my name and would call out to me as I passed. In turn, I learned a few of their names. Warren, Jasmine, and Jessica were the ones who seemed to anticipate my visits, calling out to me until I waved.

Around the first corner, Jasmine rocked back and forth in her wheelchair in the hallway.

"Hi, Jasmine."

"Hello. Do I know you?" She reached forward to clasp my hands, despite my books.

I sighed. "It's Tori. We met before."

"You remind me of my goddaughter. She's beautiful."

A nurse with a sympathetic face swooped in. "Jasmine, let's get you down to the rec hall for music."

"Oh, I love music."

"Let's go, then." The nurse swiveled Jasmine's chair in the opposite direction and disappeared around a corner.

"Knock, knock," I called out, before actually rapping on Marigold's doorframe. I couldn't wait to plug in the diffusing scent machine so it smelled more like cinnamon in her room and less like the rest of Willow Springs.

From her recliner, Marigold's eyes fluttered open. "Victoria Grace! It is fantastic to see you today."

Every time she greeted me, I felt important, like a princess. I deposited my books onto our table next to the giant window. "I know. I thought I'd stop by and keep you company while I work on my homework."

"Splendid." She pushed her bony shoulders up with a groan. "This old body isn't quite what it used to be. Would you reach into the top drawer of my bureau and get my peppermint oil?"

Having no idea what a bureau was, I pulled open the top drawer of the little stand near her bed. Lotions, medicine-looking tubes, and lip balms rattled around while I searched the labels. As I found the peppermint oil, a butter-colored piece of stationery underneath the hodgepodge caught my eye. It had no lines and tiny yellow flowers bordered the sides. Black slanting cursive was crossed off here and there.

"Did you find it?"

"Uh, yes." I pulled the oil and note from the drawer and placed both in her lap. "What's this?"

"Horsefeathers," she whispered, taking the paper into her hands. "You shouldn't snoop in private matters, dear."

"You're the one who told me to get into the drawer."

Marigold glanced up to me, the paper still in her hands. "True, but you should mind your own business." She folded the piece of paper along the well-worn crease. Her head bowed.

"I'm sorry." Great. I was a walking ball of hate and discontent. "I'll...I'll just go." Seemed like the day was just waiting to kick me in the teeth. I gathered my books, my teeth clamped together. Corbin was still waiting for me to send him a text too.

"Victoria Grace, sit." Marigold shifted herself forward, one hand extended to my empty chair.

I obeyed, books still clutched to my chest for a quick exit in case things continued to go south.

"I apologize, too." She smoothed the paper open onto the table. "No one has ever seen this before. I put it away years ago, when I moved here, and it startled me to see it again." The veins in her hands bulged bright blue. "This is my to-do list." She stopped her movements and looked up at me.

I held my breath. Was I supposed to ask a question or say something?

"After my mistress died, I lost who I was, my purpose. I had always been with her until she died. Suddenly, I was alone. I was overseas, in an empty apartment, while her family settled her affairs. No friends, no family." Marigold petted the pale paper. "I walked the streets of Paris and observed life in the streets. I had always been at my mistress' whim, able to do whatever she wanted, whenever she called. It's hard to admit now that my best friend had me on her payroll."

Paris? "Did you get to see the Eiffel Tower?"

Her laughter filled the room. "Dear child, we saw it from the hotel window every day."

I couldn't even imagine seeing the infamous framework stretching into the skyline. "That's so cool."

"It was fabulous. Especially at night." Marigold flattened the paper again. "But, when you're sad and alone, it's only a brown piece of metal." She refolded the list. "I walked the sidewalks, ate baguettes, drank wine. I ordered things from the menu I'd always wanted to try, things my mistress wouldn't tolerate. You see, she rarely left the apartment. I sorted through her wardrobe and went for days without makeup."

She skimmed the paper before turning her attention to the picture on her dresser. "I'd been with her since I was sixteen, living as a shadow, bending to the will of everyone else. One day, at no particular café at all, I wrote a list of everything I wanted to do before I died. I was seventy-one and no spring chicken myself." Marigold paused and shifted her gaze to me. "Someday, a long time from now, I hope you have much less sorrow than I do."

I nodded, hoping she'd continue. It worked.

"This list holds my regrets, things I wanted to do but never did. A few I was able to finish, like finding Harold's and Kenny's tombs at Arlington. Or living in a cabin for a month with no electricity or phones."

"Running water?" No showers? Ew.

She giggled. "That was my one requirement. And it was peaceful." Her pale eyes turned to the window, and she stared far beyond the atrium.

My phone vibrated in my pocket. I ignored it, but the sound made Marigold return to the room.

"But I'll never be able to complete the list, and I came to terms with that the day I put it in my bureau drawer."

"Why can't you finish?"

Her eyes flicked from my face to the paper and back again. "It is out of my hands. In particular, this one." A crooked finger pointed to one of the two uncrossed items: "My family."

"Your family?"

"When I came to Los Angeles, no one knew where I came from or who I was. World War II was starting, and my older brother, Harold, enlisted and was stationed in Glendale. He was never deployed, but he died in an accident on the base."

I had to be missing a piece of the puzzle, and I waited in silence.

"Could you fetch me water, please?"

Agh! I wanted the story but retrieved her a fresh glass and carefully lowered myself into the chair.

She took a long draw. "Good job, Victoria Grace. You sat like a proper lady."

"Thank you." Hey! I was a lady!

"I hope you will never know the sting of prejudice, dear. It is vicious and hateful and poisons everything in your life." Marigold inhaled deeply. "No one knew that I was, that I *am*, half Japanese. And during World War II, particularly in California, it was not a good thing to be Japanese."

My brain scrambled for history lessons, coming up with nada.

"Rumors spread and the government put many Japanese families in internment camps, my own family included."

"They don't teach us this in history class."

She nodded while taking another drink. "I sent the last money transfer to my mother on the morning of December 7, 1941, my twenty-first birthday. We were listening to the 11:30 *World News Today* radio broadcast when we learned about Pearl Harbor. Japanese families were rounded up within weeks. Some were charged as spies. They disappeared by the bus full. Neither Harold nor I ever heard from our mother or younger brother or sisters again. And then I lost Harold too."

What was that book? The one about the Great Depression and the endless car ride across the country? I felt like I was in the middle of reading a weird book like that, only Marigold was the storyteller.

"How did you find out they were put into a camp?"

"I sent a letter to a neighbor, asking her to read the letter to

Mother, since she hadn't bought new glasses. She didn't need glasses, but it was the only thing I could think of to not raise suspicion. Mrs. Hudson wrote back to me, to a post office box in my maiden name. They had been taken away, even little Thomas." Her voice hitched and tears crowded her wrinkled eyelids. "Mrs. Hudson asked where I was living, and I suspect she wanted to turn me in. I destroyed the letter and closed the box." There was no mistaking her bitterness.

I wanted to reach back through time and hunt Mrs. Hudson down. "How horrible."

"For the circumstances, no. The Japanese killed many servicemen, and people back home needed someone to hate. I happened to share their genetics. My blue eyes that my brother teased me so much about while growing up saved my life."

My heart battered around inside my ribcage. "Do you know what happened to your mom and brothers and sisters?" I asked, craving to know, yet not wanting to hear the heartache.

"Much later, I learned illness was rampant in their camp. They died within the first year of pneumonia and reactions to the vaccinations."

Everyone in her family was dead. "Miss Marigold, I'm so sorry." I pushed my words out, despite the lump in my throat.

"When I say I'm alone, Victoria Grace, it is in every sense of the word." Her eyes were full of unshed tears. "You have brought a ray of sunshine into my last days."

My face warmed. I'd never been anyone's sunshine. "But you still have time to see if there is any more information about them. There's lots of research online."

"Sweet child, they are gone. Nothing I find will change that."

"What if they survived the illness? Or I could find where they were buried."

She sighed. "Thank you for your hope."

I whipped my notebook from my backpack and opened it. "What are their names?"

"There is no deterring you." Marigold took a deep, rattling breath. "Well, there was Harold and then me. Next came Daisy, Lily, Rosie, and baby Thomas."

After I scratched down all the names, I whistled. "Six kids. That's a pack."

"One of our neighbors had nine."

"Your mom liked flowers."

A smile blossomed across her thin lips. "She did. She had a beautiful garden. It was her favorite place to be."

"Were your brothers named after your dad?"

"They were. Harold was Father's given name and Thomas was his middle name. He met my mother when he was on a missions trip to Japan after World War I."

A vision of Zach and Jack wrestling popped into my mind. "What was it like with a lot of siblings?"

"Busy." She chuckled and took a sip of water. "Always busy. We went to school and worked at home. The girls made meals and worked in the vegetable garden. Harold learned to hunt. He also worked at the packing plant after school was out for the day and during the summer."

"I think we have a program in our library to look up ancestry stuff." Directly in the middle, protected by bookworms and nerds.

"You won't find anything, Victoria Grace."

I turned her list toward me. "It seems a bit more reachable than...skydiving?"

Marigold laughed until she coughed. "Well, I did trick riding as a kid, and I thought it wouldn't be too bad to try."

I could totally envision the frail woman across from me strapped to a skydiving instructor, grinning the entire drop out of the clear blue sky.

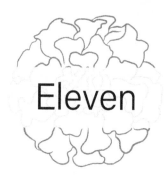

Eleven

BY THE TIME MAMABEAR PICKED ME UP, I'D ALREADY finished my homework, sent a text to Madison asking for details about homecoming, and talked Corbin into meeting me at my locker to introduce him to Madison. Better to know two kids in Butte than one. Besides, if I delayed their meet and greet, Mads would pounce him at lunch.

MamaBear and I were mowing through our favorite Chinese take-out and watching *Breakfast at Tiffany's* for the millionth time when my phone whistled.

"You gotta get a new ringtone for that guy." MamaBear didn't even have to see the screen to know it was Corbin. She had mad detective skills.

Corbin: The moving company spilled something weird on the two boxes of clothes I own. I'm stuck doing laundry.

Ha! A guy who can do his own laundry. That's impressive.

My favorite part was on, when Holly and Paul were in the five-and-dime store. I wouldn't even attempt to steal anything. I'd probably get caught. Then, I'd cry while confessing.

Corbin: I am pretty impressive, now that I think about it.

I'm changing my contact name. You're now "The Impressive Corbin"

The Impressive Corbin: Such an honor. I'd like to thank the

Academy, my director, my agent, and God. You can't even see the way I pointed to the sky when I said that.

Your title is too long. I'll abbreviate it to TIC

TIC: And you could be TAC and then it'd be sweet.

I see what you did there.

My controlling nature got the best of me, and I changed back his contact name.

"You're gonna miss the movie."

"Mom. I've seen it approximately six hundred fifty-seven times."

She snorted. "Are you sure that is an accurate approximation, ma'am?"

"This is not a court of law. I'm not under oath." I squealed when her finger dug into my hip. "I'm gonna spit chicken fried rice on you!"

"You know where the vacuum is." MamaBear swapped our cartons. "Shift change is coming up. I am switching to working weekends, since Christmas is on a Tuesday and Thanksgiving is on a Thursday."

"Ironically, it's on Thursday every year," I said, leaning away from her.

"Pipe down over there." She flung her legs across my lap, and I had to hold my chow mein in the air to keep it from flying everywhere. "Looks like we can start house shopping at the beginning of the year."

Punch hyperdrive, to the sound of my screech of joy. We'd never lived in anything other than rentals. "Two or three bedrooms? Can we have a pool? And a dog?"

"Two. No and no because I am going to apply to be a K9 handler."

"We need to celebrate! Let's go get ice cream. I'll buy."

MamaBear chuckled into the rice. "Save your pennies for a car, kid. We should be able to make that happen before Christmas, January at the latest."

I jumped up from the couch and plunked my carton on the kitchen counter. "Shiny, happy unicorns!" Without much effort, I shouted above the television volume. "Fluffy, lucky rabbits."

MamaBear laughed as I wiggled my body to my own music. "You're blocking my view! Sit!"

"I get a car," I sang. "We get a house. And you get a dog that bites bad guys. Best. Year. Ever!" I was dizzy from spinning before I realized she didn't seem as happy as she should be. "What's wrong, Mr. Grumpy Gills?"

She took a measured breath, stood, and placed her rice next to my noodles on the counter. "I need to let you know that your dad came by while you were at Marigold's." Her shoulders slumped forward.

"My what did what?" I must've misheard what she said because that particular male lived in Colorado and had zero to do with my life.

"David came by earlier."

Yeah, I heard that right. "Why?"

Slowly, ever so slowly, MamaBear turned. Her hands landed near her waist, where her gun belt usually sat—the first place she reached for when things weren't going well. "The court order finally caught up with him. He came to ask if I would drop it."

"Wow." I pushed my fingers through my hair. "He's such a… wow. Hasn't paid a dime in child support, like ever, and wants you to…wait, did you say yes?" For half a second, I doubted the woman responsible for my entire life.

"Tori, you know me better than that. No." She mimicked my motions and dragged her own hands through her hair, uncharacteristically loosened from its regular ponytail. Lips pressed together, she forced out a breath. "I told him it would go toward your car and college."

I asked the million-dollar question. "Did he even ask about me?"

Her hesitation told me the answer.

Angry tears spilled over. "I'm glad I wasn't here. I don't want to hear his excuses or get another five dollars."

"Tori..."

I pushed past her and fled to my room and resisted slamming the door. I didn't need her barging in and biting off my head for being mad at the man who still signed my late birthday cards as "Dad." He wasn't my dad—he didn't deserve that title.

Instead of crying until I gave myself a massive headache, I dumped my backpack and rearranged the contents. In the kitchen, I could hear MamaBear washing dishes with a bit more force than necessary. I was purging old Spanish notes when my phone whistled.

Corbin: Okay. Your locker is inside, right? Cause in Texas, they were all inside.

Old school, literally. Lockers are indoors. I'll wait for you near the parking lot, if it makes it easier.

Corbin: I feel like a dork. I went to the same schools growing up in Liberty Hill. I was never the new kid.

Not even at the high school?

Corbin: No. Mom taught there. I practically grew up roaming the halls. Kids thought I was cute.

I would've thought you were homeless.

The irritated sounds stopped in the kitchen. MamaBear's steps slowed outside of my bedroom door. She knocked lightly and cracked open the door. "Sorry I messed up all of the good news. Guess I should've started with the bad news first."

"No. I mean, it wouldn't have mattered." I remained on the floor. "Can I help you look at houses?"

"Sure. I'll check with one of the ladies in the church who is a realtor. Once we have a few lined up, we'll take a few tours."

I nodded and shoved my history book into my backpack. "Gotta finish up and wash my face."

MamaBear surveyed my room. "Do you think you could clean this up a bit?"

I followed her gaze. My unmade bed had the comforter wedged against the wall and a blanket drooping to the floor. Tyler Joseph was still folded in half. My dirty laundry heap could hide a small child, and the contents of my closet spilled out in wrinkled layers and shoestrings. "I guess."

"Night, spawn. Get some sleep."

"Night, Mom. I hope you get the K9 position." She'd always wanted to apply but needed a secure yard before she could take on a dog.

"Me too, although it'll be a boatload of training."

"And a pay raise." I wiggled my eyebrows.

"Wash your face, little piggy. Then clean your sty."

I oinked at her.

———— ⊢ • ⊢ ————

My foul mood returned the next morning when I realized the milk had expired. David Weston was like finding sour milk when I wanted a glass of ice cold moo juice. But at least my alarm made sure I was on time for the rendezvous with Corbin.

His Mustang rumbled through the parking lot, past the hybrids and imports. That car made me seriously jealous.

I picked my way through the careless drivers to meet him halfway. "Excuse me!" My outburst at the kid who nearly ran over my foot made Corbin raise his brows.

"Got a burr in your britches?" He loped next to me, dodging cars and kids.

"Yeah, just feeling like my cat peed in my cereal." Did I want to go down this rabbit hole with a guy who was practically a stranger? I rubbed my forehead with one hand. "My sperm donor stopped by the apartment and talked with my mom when I was at Marigold's yesterday."

"I'm guessing by your tone that he's either recently paroled from prison or you don't like him."

"I wish he was in prison."

"Um, okay." Clearly, he hadn't expected my reply.

We stopped on the sidewalk outside of the hallway with my locker. Madison didn't even know about my dad and I preferred to keep it that way. She had a way of "accidentally" sharing private information. With everyone.

"He took off when I was two. Left a note saying that he wasn't ready to be a dad." I paused and swallowed. There was no way I was going to cry, even if they were tears of anger. David already made me cry once. I wasn't going to do it again.

"Harsh," Corbin said.

"Pretty much. We found out he remarried and started a new family a few states over. Apparently, we weren't convenient for him." My lips spit out the information before my brain could tell it to shut up.

Corbin's Adam's apple bobbed up and down. "You don't talk with him?"

"Nope. He's never called. He used to send me a birthday card with a five-dollar bill." I scoffed because it sounded incredibly pitiful when admitted aloud. "Five dollars, like I'm still a baby. I've never kept any of it. I put it in the offering at church."

"That's a good idea." He scratched his head before proceeding with caution. "And he came by the apartment and your mom was there?"

"Yup. Wanted her to rescind the court order going after child support. She filed it seven years ago, and he's avoided it since then by working odd jobs and deferring court rulings."

He was silent. I kept going.

"I mean, he was the one who left us high and dry. Mom had to borrow money to pay for rent and food. She put herself through school to become an officer." My hands were shaking.

"I'm sorry."

"It's…it's not okay. I mean, you don't have to apologize. He was the one who abandoned us and started over."

"Do you talk to your half-brothers or sisters?"

"No. If I do, I seriously doubt they know I exist." And there it was, out in the open. As the words passed my lips, tears bunched into the corners of my eyes. "It's just fantastic to be forgotten by your own dad," I whispered, blinking fast.

"I miss my dad. He taught me to ride a horse and drive the four-wheeler."

"He sounds wonderful." I was jealous and heartbroken at the same time. "What was his name?"

"Michael. Michael Dallas. He was even taller than I am, six foot ten. And everyone called him Little Mikey."

"Six foot ten? How tall was your mom?"

"Well, the sad part is I don't exactly remember. She was tall, maybe your height."

"And her name?"

"Hannah."

"How'd they meet?" I could imagine being in a family like this—a dad, mom, and little sister. They probably ate dinner together every night and knew how to make homemade ice cream.

"College summer camp counselors."

"Sounds like a fairy tale or Hallmark movie."

"They were pretty sappy. Still held hands whenever we went to town. Katie hated it when they kissed in front of her. She'd cover her eyes and gag."

"Your sister?"

"Yeah. She was nine."

I felt like my gut had been elbowed. Forever nine years old. "I didn't mean to pry."

"Sometimes, it feels like it was a movie. I was a kid in a horrible movie and they were never real." His words choked. "But when it's all said and done, I'm lucky to have had them for that long. Some people don't even get to know their parents. And nobody ever talks about mine anymore." He gazed down at me, a tear spilling from his eye.

I leaned my head forward to his chest and cried. I'd come to him so angry, needing to vent, and he turned it around to make me feel almost pitiful for my dad.

"He chose to leave me," I muttered into Corbin's T-shirt. He smelled like laundry detergent, with a hint of cologne.

"He's a downright idiot."

Part of me wanted to peek up at Corbin to see if he was watching me. Would it be like a movie scene and he'd lean down and kiss me?

What was I thinking? I barely knew him and he was a friend.

The practical side of me dragged my sleeve across my runny nose and I stepped backwards. He was the only guy who seemed interesting in the otherwise-stale genetic pool of Redding. There was no chance I'd let the random, gooey feeling in the pit of my stomach ruin this new friendship.

And friends wiped their snotty noses in front of one another. Plus, I suddenly was nervous—I'd never cried in front of a guy, let alone rested against his muscular chest. Yeah, I could feel those muscles under the cotton shirt.

Someone shoved me toward the double doors as the first bell sounded. I hiccupped. "Now that I'm all blotchy from crying, let's go start your first day at Butte High."

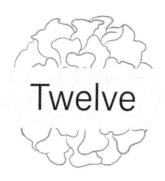

Twelve

MY DAYS FELL INTO A COMFORTABLE PATTERN. I'D MEET Corbin at the parking lot before school. We talked Lucy Garden into switching seats so we could sit next to each other in second period. At lunch, Madison would pester Corbin into saying words with his drawl. Our phones would alternately blow up or go silent if I was working or with Marigold. At youth group, we'd foot race for the chair, cheating allowed.

The week after Halloween, I stopped in for a quick hello before my shift, dashing past Jasmine when she was distracted. My surprise for Marigold arrived the day before, and I couldn't wait to show her.

"Victoria Grace, I could hear your feet slapping all the way down the hallway." She sat like a queen in her bed, surrounded by her pillowed subjects.

I laughed, shucking my backpack to my chair. "I have to hurry because my shift starts early." She was going to love what I bought for us.

"What does your shirt say? 'This is my costume.'"

Reading my shirt upside down, I shrugged. "I don't do Halloween."

"But it was last week, dear." She shook her head. "Pity for you. You've never been to a masquerade, have you?"

"Nope. Not many of those in Redding."

Marigold's eyebrows stretched up. "Paris, 1956 on the mistress' whim. She played the musical saw."

"The kind you cut trees with?"

She giggled. "The very same." Her eyes shifted to my hands, still hidden in my backpack. "What have you got there?"

I couldn't even help my grin and squeal. "I ordered this a couple of weeks ago and it finally came." Pulling out the shipping box, I placed it into her lap and clapped my hands.

Marigold tugged the tape deliberately, agonizingly slow. I tapped my foot until she glared at me. Finally, she pulled out the flowered box from within, and I snapped away the ugly shipping package.

"Open it!" I was like a two-year-old, knowing what was coming, impatient with anticipation.

Soon, beautiful pale yellow stationery appeared, bordered with tiny marigolds. Matching envelopes were bound with an orange ribbon. Our first names were blazed in gold calligraphy across the bottom of each yellow paper: Marigold and Tori.

"Now we can write to Nick and his unit!" I pulled out my laptop and brought up the website I needed. "This is the agency we picked before. I already emailed them, sent our picture, and let them know our idea. Nicky doesn't have his address yet, but we can get a care package started while we work on letters."

My fingers were flying around the screen, pointing out highlights and contact information before I realized Marigold had stilled. I froze when I saw the tears in her eyes. Did I mess up the names?

"Victoria Grace, you are a miracle." She patted my hand.

"Thought I heard you in here." Sheila filled the doorway, smile in place. "What are you two up to?"

I bit my lip to stay silent while Marigold explained our upcoming task, using small hand motions. "I will need to clear a shelf for our supplies," she said, nodding toward the sink. Anything but the snack cupboard.

"I'll get someone in here to help you decide on that after dinner, Miss Marigold. I've gotta shoot to the dining hall. See you in a bit." Sheila inclined her head toward me. "I'll see you soon, then, unless you're staying for turkey gravy."

"Sorry. Working in fifteen minutes, and I have to take off."

Marigold handed the stationery back to me, and I arranged it on our table at the window. The buttercup-colored paper made my heart happy.

"Travel safely, Victoria Grace. It's darker now."

"I will. I'll be back tomorrow before I have to go to work and we can start on our letters."

When I pedaled into the theater parking lot, Mr. Bolt was on the other side of the glass panes, holding out a drawing to a woman surrounded by paint cans. While a cynic in most other parts of my life, I took my Christmas decorating seriously. This year, Mr. Bolt held a contest for employees to submit artwork for the entryway. Mine was a mash-up of super heroes and cartoon characters having a snowball fight.

"Tori!" Mr. Bolt's cheerful greeting made me cautious the moment I entered the lobby. He was never chipper. He waved me over to the painter. "Tori, this is Amy. She will be painting your drawing on the windows this year. Well done!" Mr. Bolt vigorously pumped my palm up and down with his damp hand.

"I should go clock in so that I'm not late." I pulled back from the bizarre, over-the-top congratulations. I hustled to the break room, wiping my palm on my pants. Technically, if my hours held, I'd only have to work through the end of the year to get my car. Then, I could hunt for a job a tad more classy than wrestling overflowing trash cans and picking gum from carpets.

There was enough time to send a couple of texts. Group texts were plain annoying. I copied and pasted the message twice.

Guess who's drawing is currently getting painted on the front of the theater?

MamaBear: Mr. Bolt's

Corbin: Aubrey
Corbin: Rosie
Corbin: Mr. Bolt

Dorks. I smiled and powered down my phone. The shift blasted by, helped along by a blockbuster romantic comedy and a cartoon sequel. Missing my breaks meant a little bit of overtime pay. But I drowned in kiddie popcorn trash thrown under every single chair. What kind of parent let their kids become monkeys in a theater? Ones who never had fifteen minutes to sweep before their boss had a hissy fit, that's who.

A few minutes after midnight, I unlocked my bike from the rack and nearly jumped out of my skin when a patrol car rolled up next to me and hit the siren yelp button.

"That's not even funny," I gasped, glaring at MamaBear.

She grinned. "Oh, but it was. Want an escort?"

"I want a ride."

"Hang on, lemme call my sergeant."

My breath curled up to my forehead. I should've listened to her this morning and packed a beanie. At least I had gloves and it wasn't raining.

The trunk popped open and she got out. "Let me get junk out of the way."

My coworkers walked to their cars. A few waved while others refused to make eye contact. "I don't want to go to jail," I yelled, for the benefit of the latter.

"Ma'am, you need to pipe down or I'll ground you." MamaBear moved to the front seat and rearranged her gear to make room for me.

Normally, I loved listening to the chatter on the police radio, but it was silent. "How's your shift?" Anyone who loves anyone in law enforcement never, *ever* mentions the word "quiet." It causes hate and discontent to rise up for the rest of the shift.

"One report down. Can't complain." She cranked up the heater. "I like your windows."

"I didn't even know I'd won until I walked in and Mr. Bolt gave me a slimy handshake." I told her about his unexpected excitement.

She pulled into the apartment parking lot and up to our sidewalk. It wouldn't be too soon before we were packing up and leaving. Every Wednesday morning at 5:30, my alarm clock was a dumpster slamming into the trash truck. I wouldn't miss that.

She leaned across the small laptop and kissed my forehead. "Love you. Get out."

"I pay your wages. Love you, too." I couldn't resist teasing her with the same phrase irate citizens, usually in handcuffs, would yell in her face. Obviously, they didn't know it would not help their situation.

"You're grounded forever. Go to bed."

———— ◦ ————

The weather in Redding is freakish. Stuck between a few mountain ranges, it can be raining one day and over a hundred degrees two days later. Such was the case the next morning. I checked the weather app and it was nearly eighty degrees at ten in the morning. Then I noticed I had three texts, the first one shortly after 3 a.m.

MamaBear: You snore. But it's cute.

I smiled at the screen. She adamantly refused to admit that she was guilty of the same thing. At least I acknowledged it.

Corbin: Let me know when you're up.

Why had he sent a text at six in the morning? Freak. His next one was a few hours later.

Corbin: I forgot you didn't get off until this morning. Hope I didn't wake you.

Barely awake. What's up?

I stretched in bed and wished I had a butler to bring me breakfast.

Corbin: Want to meet up for coffee?

Sure. Give me 45 mins. The place near Willow Springs okay? That way, I could walk across the street to work on the letters. **Corbin: Sounds good.**

I showered and pilfered a bit of money to buy scones. The coffee shop's almond scones were delicious goodness and worth every penny. I grabbed enough money for two. Maybe Corbin would like a scone. Maybe he wouldn't, but at least I could ask and then pay for it. He'd probably be all cowboy and pay for both of ours. But it was better to have the money just in case.

Someday, I figured I'd go to a makeup counter at a department store and learn how to put on fancy eyeshadow. But for now I was grateful I didn't have a giant pimple on my nose. I swiped on mascara and a tiny bit of lip gloss before I let MamaBear know my schedule. At least I'd learned to keep my mouth closed while applying mascara—something I'd worked on since hearing a man on the radio mock his girlfriend for opening her mouth in a "stupid 'O' shape."

Meeting up with Corbin for coffee, then Willow Springs. Work from 6-1. Love ya.

MamaBear: Back at the station now. If it's not busy, I'll see you around 1.

I flew down the streets, hot air flapping my vintage Audio Adrenaline concert shirt. Well, it technically was MamaBear's, but I stole it a few years before. My damp hair helped cool me down but was nearly dry by the time I arrived at the coffee shop.

Corbin leaned against his Mustang, flipping through his phone screen. It surprised me to see him in an unbuttoned, long sleeve shirt over a tank top with jeans and tennis shoes. I focused on pulling up to the bike rack instead of on his biceps.

He stashed his phone into his back pocket. "It's hot. Why in the world are you wearing shoes and socks and not flip-flops?"

"You're not wearing flip-flops."

"They don't exactly fit on my metal foot. Why don't you wear them?"

Not my favorite subject. "Because I have deformed toes."

"Wait, what?"

I could feel my cheeks heat up, and not from the radiant asphalt. "My second and third toes on my left foot are fused at the base."

"Really?"

"Why in the world would I make up something like that when I'd rather be in sandals? Or even have a pedicure for once in my life?" I shouldn't have been irritated at his question, but I was. It wasn't my fault my toes were stuck together.

"Didn't that Olympic swimmer have fused toes? Michael Phelps."

The amount of times that factoid had been thrown at me was ridiculous. But still, Corbin was trying. "Yeah, he does. But I'm not much of a swimmer."

Corbin knocked his metal shin and held the front door open. "I'm a bit lopsided myself."

Of course, he paid for everything, even my scone. He crossed his arms and flat out refused to let me repay him. "It's a drink and a pastry."

"Not a pastry, a scone. A delectable, yummy scone. You sure you don't want a bite?" I broke off a corner and extended it to him.

"Sure. Thanks." He leaned his head back and popped the whole thing into his mouth. "What are you and Marigold up to?"

"Writing letters to soldiers deployed overseas for Christmas. We got our own fancy stationery and everything."

He took a long draw from his iced coffee. "Didn't you finish up your credits a while ago?"

"Pretty much. I like hanging out with her. She helped me get an A on my history papers."

"I'll have to swing by and meet her."

"You should. But not today, because we have to start our letters and she'll talk your ear off about living in Hollywood or Paris or asking you questions about how you grew up," I said, standing up.

Corbin stood and chucked his empty cup into the trash. "All right. Y'all will have to put me in your appointment book."

"Next week. You can swing by then." I shoved the door open before he could get to it. "And no ambushing me at the theater." I pushed my bike across the street to Willow Springs.

"No promises," he called out.

Marigold's room was ice-cold from the air conditioning and radiated the smell of cinnamon. She was already in her armchair, crocheted blankets draped over her shoulders and legs. "It gets chilly with the air on."

I fanned my face. "It's better than the oven outside. You ready to start on the letters?"

"They are in the cupboard above the sink."

Fantastic. The cupcakes were safe. I reached up to grab the stationery.

"Do you have a young man?"

I froze and felt my cheeks burn with embarrassment. "Um, no." That was random.

"Well, you should…someday. Not now, but someday. He doesn't need to be handsome, although it is a nice benefit." She cleared her throat. "Make sure he is worthy. Don't settle for anyone. Settling is living in fear, and a life lived in fear is a life half-lived."

"Did you settle?" The words tumbled out before I thought it through. I turned away and felt like an idiot until she spoke.

"I did. I regretted it every day of my life." Marigold's voice was low, barely above a whisper. "Oh, I wish I could undo that decision. But I would never do that because then I wouldn't have met you, my dear." The remorse that had seeped into her voice fled and was replaced with joy. "I wouldn't trade having your acquaintance for all the tea in China."

My smile crept up slowly. I was like warm, yummy tea. Hurray for tea! With stationery in hand, I sat down at our table. On the back of the invoice from the seller, I jotted down notes of what we wanted to say—nothing too cheesy or too sentimental. Definitely wanted to make sure the soldiers understood our gratitude for serving away from their families during the holidays.

I'd finished scribbling out the rough draft when there was a knock on the metal doorframe. Corbin still had his hand in the air when I looked up.

"Can we help you?" Marigold's question made me smirk.

"Yes, ma'am." He took a step inside the room. "Tori forgot her phone, and I'm sure she'd like it before she goes to work." Corbin held my green-cased phone out in his big hand.

I stood up and met him near the foot of the bed. "Thanks."

"I waited for you to come back but figured you didn't realize you'd left it behind."

Marigold cleared her throat.

Ah, my cue. "Miss Marigold Williams, this is Corbin Dallas. He goes to my youth group and school." I sat back down. If the two of them got talking, I'd never get the letters started. We needed to get them mailed to the agency in the next couple of weeks to make sure the soldiers got them by Christmas.

He strode to her chair and gently took her hand. "It's a pleasure, ma'am."

"Likewise, Mr. Dallas. From the sounds of it, you aren't from around here."

"No, ma'am. Texan, born and bred." He glanced up at me with a wink. Wait. Why'd he wink? "But I know you two are up to something important, so I'll leave you to it." He squeezed her hand and sauntered out the door.

He'd barely turned down the hallway when Marigold grinned and wiggled her eyebrows. "That boy is a tall drink of water."

Thirteen

THE VARSITY BASKETBALL COACH INVITED ME TO OPEN gym the following week. Since tryouts were the week before Thanksgiving, I figured the extra exposure couldn't hurt. After school on Monday, I pushed in my earbuds and shot around with seven other girls on one side of the gym, while gangly freshmen boys occupied the other half. I hustled to Marigold's afterwards and focused on my handwriting; it was awful next to her looping, graceful cursive.

Tuesday, MamaBear gave me and my bike a ride to school because the rain returned. Crazy weather. I stuffed a jacket through the loops of my backpack so I'd be dry for the ride to Marigold's later. Well, mostly dry.

Mads and Josh were on the outs again. Corbin and I heard the blow-by-blow during lunch.

"He never listens to me." She stuck out her bottom lip, with a theatrical sigh. "I'm entirely done with him."

Corbin hid his grin behind his bottle of Gatorade. We'd heard the same argument three, no, four days before. "Ya don't say?"

I elbowed him through his denim jacket.

"I'm serious this time, guys."

I was saved from a lame answer by the bell ringing. Madison left us at the lockers, deleting photos from her phone as she strode away.

"You have basketball again today?" Corbin pulled his beanie off, shook his hair, then tugged the black knit cap back on. Did he ever go to his locker?

"Yeah, then Marigold's. We're almost finished with the letters." I grabbed my Nutrition book and slammed the locker door. "Tuesday night is high-stakes poker for you with Grammy and Aunt Sue, right?"

He laughed. "You're jealous you don't know how to play."

I skipped every other step on the staircase to the second floor and yelled over my shoulder, "Sorry. I can't hear you from up here."

The afternoon trudged by. I didn't even have time to see Corbin or Madison before Coach Neems cornered me in the hallway at the final bell and escorted me to the locker room, Lit book and all. He wanted to go over the plays for the varsity team.

My new playlist on my phone helped block the distractions, namely wanting to see Corbin. I needed this season to go well, to have the stats to support my scholar/athlete scholarship applications. If I didn't start, I needed to be the go-to sub. I focused on my free throws while the other girls fiddled with three pointers.

Out of the corner of my eye, I saw Corbin leaning in the doorway, one shoulder hiked higher to keep his backpack in place. My shot banged off the backboard. It was hard enough sharing the gym with the freshmen boys' team without the tall distraction. When had he become eye candy? And why was I thinking my friend was hot? What was wrong with me? Seriously.

When Coach blew the whistle, I was relieved. My personal shadow disappeared from the door, but I had a feeling he was nearby. I switched shoes and grabbed my bag. Hopefully it wasn't raining.

No such luck. I heard the downpour before I even reached the lobby. At least Marigold had an extra towel.

Corbin pushed off of the lobby wall as I left the gym. "Hey." His beanie was gone, replaced by a faded baseball cap, pulled low.

I tucked stray hair back after I pulled on my hoodie. "Hey."

"Want a ride?"

Let's see…showered in my clothes with running mascara, or dry car? "Yeah. I'm going to Marigold's."

"I know."

"Wait—where's my bike?" Even through the wall of water, I saw the bike rack between the parking lot and the gymnasium entrance was empty.

"I put it in my car." He hooked his thumb into a belt loop.

"You're handy."

We sprinted to his Mustang. "It's open," he yelled when we got close.

For some reason, the situation was entirely hilarious and I laughed while we ran, until we slammed the doors closed. Maybe it was the rain or the fact that I was drenched and water dripped off of Corbin's chin.

I shoved my soaking hair from my forehead. "Thanks for the lift. This would've been unfortunate to ride my bike in."

"No problem." Corbin turned the key, and the 351 Windsor V8 engine roared to life. I could feel the vibration through the torn vinyl seat. It smelled like hay and grease in the cab.

"Oh, I covet this car." Even the faded paint and the woodgrain steering wheel.

"You wouldn't covet the amount of gas it uses." The wipers squeaked across the windshield. "Or the time you meant to get new wiper blades and forgot." Water smeared back and forth.

"It's better than a bike."

"It's more expensive than a bike."

"It's drier than a bike," I countered.

He backed out of the parking spot while I shot off a text to MamaBear.

Got a ride from Corbin to Marigold's. Hurray for a dry car! I want a dry car.

She sent me a crying emoji.

MamaBear: STBY

"My mom is the worst."

He flipped his blinker on, waiting for the light to turn. "Why's that?"

"I'm so close on my half of the car payment. I told her that I want a car, and she said, 'Sucks to be you.'"

Corbin burst out laughing. "She actually said that?"

I flipped the screen toward his face. "Yeah, that's what those four letters mean."

"Well, I can give you a ride, if you want." He fiddled with the heater knob. "When your mom can't take you."

"Sweet! I'll get to pretend I'm your..." The word stuck in my throat. I wasn't, nor had plans to become, his girlfriend. My brain was a traitor. "Sidekick."

The wipers whined across the windshield. Talk about open mouth, insert foot. I had to change the topic quick. "Thanks for the ride."

"No problem." He pulled a pack of gum from his jacket pocket and held it out for me to choose.

I didn't like fruit-flavored gum in particular, but picked one. "You don't have to give me a ride on rainy days. I won't melt, despite what they say about me."

Corbin eased the Mustang into Willow Springs. "Do I need a reason to help a pretty girl in a wet hoodie?" He got out before I could answer and opened the trunk.

My heart stammered. He called me pretty. Was that a big deal? Or was he being nice?

I shouldered my backpack and walked to the back of the Mustang. The downpour slowed to a steady rain.

Keeping my head down out of sheer awkwardness, I grabbed my bike as soon as he set it on the pavement, careful not to touch his hand. "Thank you." It was the only thing I could manage to say out loud before I did an awkward run-fast-walk thing into the building. The engine idled as I hurried toward the lobby.

I glanced back and saw him watch me until the door closed.

Safely behind the glass, I waited until he inched his car out of the parking lot.

My scrambled brain stretched like a rubber band with possibilities and what he meant, then snapped back to reality. It wasn't anything. He was a polite guy and it was in his nature to compliment people. I mean, he liked to tell Madison every day that she looked pretty. And the realization slammed my thoughts into a solid brick wall—Corbin Dallas was the hero in a movie and I was his trusty sidekick. Nothing more. Call me Spock.

Nursing my pity party for one, I moped to Marigold's room, only to find it empty. I craned my head back to the hallway and checked the room number. Yes, right room number—1206. Cinnamon infused air. Cushy brown armchair with the thick blue blanket across the back. Where was she? I checked the cupboard— over half of the letters were missing.

My brain jumped to about ten horrible conclusions in five seconds while my panicked feet raced back to the front counter.

"Jamie, where's Marigold?" I gripped the laminate, bracing for the worst: heart attack, stroke… What if she was dead? My stomach dropped and I wanted to barf.

She popped her gum. "There's a meeting in the dining hall," she said with a yawn.

"Thanks." I hurried to the dining room and slid to a stop when Marigold's voice floated out from a crackling speaker.

In front of wheelchairs and more than two dozen snowy-topped senior citizens, Marigold explained our letter writing campaign into a microphone. "I know some of you like to draw or paint. Pam, I know you have a box of knitted caps. If any of you would like us to send a gift to our servicemen, Sheila will collect them…oh!" She spotted me across the sea of white tufts. "Victoria Grace, come here."

I flinched from the feedback and trotted to the front. "Hi." I waved and spotted Warren and Jessica in the crowd. Where was Jasmine?

"This is my friend, Victoria Grace Weston. Her cousin shipped out and won't be home for Christmas."

Murmurs rippled through the bobbing heads. "Such a pity." "When's dinner?" "My grandson is stationed in England."

"Would you like to say anything, Victoria?" She thrust the mic into my hand.

I held it far enough away to avoid interference squawking noise. "If you want to write a letter or a card, we can send those too." I thrust the microphone to Sheila.

She didn't need it, with a voice like that. "Okay, thirty minutes until dinner starts. Go see what you can put together for Tori and Marigold, and I'll see you in a bit."

Walkers scraped out of the double doors while others propelled their wheelchairs forward with their own slippered feet. I offered my arm to Marigold. She leaned into my ribs, her fingers digging into my skin through my long sleeves.

"That went well." Her tiny steps made me slow down to a crawl.

"Yeah, I hope they turn in some stuff we can send." Personally, I was almost dreading what exactly they would hand over. An unraveled, pilled scarf? Maybe an illegible letter.

Marigold was breathless by the time we reached her room. I helped ease her into bed and lowered her head a bit.

She sank into her pillow and sighed. "I'm so winded."

"It's okay. You lay here and catch your breath. I'll finish the rest of the letters."

Her eyes fluttered close. "Sounds lovely."

I pulled down the stationery and carefully wrote out our letter:

Dear Hero,

We hope this letter finds you safe during this holiday season. Though we do not know you personally, we are grateful for your service to our country, even more so during this time of year, when you are away from your family and loved ones.

Hopefully, we can bring you a bit of cheer with this letter. We are Marigold and Tori, a young gal in her 90s and the other in high school. Marigold wrote letters for soldiers in World War II and Tori's cousin is currently deployed, so we decided to dust off our pens and take the time to make sure to let you know that you have admirers across the miles.

You're in our prayers—for your safety and that you would find joy far from home. You are a hero in our eyes.

In advance, Merry Christmas and a Happy New Year.

My hand cramped after the final letter—fifty-two in all. I shook my fingers while I located my phone. It had been on silent and I'd missed two texts from MamaBear, a phone call from her, and a text each from both Corbin and Madison.

First things first. I swiped MamaBear's texts open.

MamaBear: Do I need to pick you up?

MamaBear: Hello?

Sorry. My phone was on silent. I've been working on the letters. Marigold is worn out and I didn't even see the time. Yes, I need a ride.

Mads: Josh totally made it up to me. Sent me these!

There were four pictures of a gigantic bouquet of red roses, followed by heart emojis. I could barely contain my sarcastic shock.

Corbin: You need a ride home?

I turned off the screen to catch a glimpse of Marigold, who had dozed off. She seemed so peaceful, while my brain bounced off the inside of my skull with his offer.

"I can hear you looking at me, dear." Her pale lips turned upwards before her eyes opened to slits. "Are you okay?"

"Yeah, I'm finishing up the letters."

She coughed into her hand and then raised the bed. "Where's Mr. Dallas? Wasn't he supposed to come this week?"

"I think he's coming Thursday. We have youth group tomorrow." I flicked my phone screen on again and sent him a reply.

Nah. MamaBear is coming to get me.

Corbin: Let me know if you need a ride in the morning.

Will do.

MamaBear: Be there in 15.

I needed something to do. If I stayed, Marigold would supernaturally pull details from me about this afternoon. "Want me to go get your dinner?"

"No. It should be here shortly. Roast beef, mashed potatoes, and a green salad."

"That sounds delicious." Our Tuesdays were usually tacos. Or waffles. Maybe cereal.

"So, my dear, will you tell me what is really on your mind? You've been fidgeting since you arrived."

I scrubbed my face with my hands and pushed my hair behind my ears. No, I did not want to tell her. But there she was, all saintly and helpful. "It's just that Corbin. Ugh. Nothing."

She chuckled. "Is it anything you have control over?"

"What?"

"You're worried about something." Marigold waved in the orderly with her dinner and waited until he left to resume. "Whatever you are worried about, do you have control over it?"

This had to be a trick question. "I don't have control over what he said, but my brain is running like a horse at the Derby."

"If you are lucky, you will grow old. Maybe you will remember this day and maybe you won't. But if you can't change whatever he said, then don't worry about it."

I don't think she remembered the ramblings of her own seventeen-year-old brain and its rampant hormonal influences. But I could try to tame my mind to not be an idiot in Corbin's presence. Besides, he wasn't the first person to call me pretty—Bob the usher did that every Sunday.

"I'll give it a go."

She arched a thin white brow at me while balancing mashed potatoes on her fork.

"Honestly, I'll try to talk myself into forgetting it ever happened." I carefully stacked the letters and put them in the cupboard. "Thursday, we'll collect everything, and I'll get it mailed by Friday."

Marigold took a dainty sip of water. "Perfect. And we'll settle in for a nice visit with Mr. Dallas."

As I walked down the hall and out to MamaBear's car, I muttered out loud to myself. "I'm the sidekick. Like Inigo and Fezzik. Or Marlin and Dory. Dwight Schrute and Michael Scott. The sidekick."

I was doomed and my brain knew it.

Fourteen

CORBIN: WON'T BE AT SCHOOL MONDAY OR TUESDAY.

My hot-sauce-laden taco stopped short of my mouth.

Are you pre-planning your illness? Or has Madison taught you her devious ways?

A bit of meat plunked onto my plate, and I swiped it up with my finger.

"Slob." MamaBear chucked a napkin at my face.

"I can't hear you through this deliciousness," I mumbled, mouth crammed with food.

Corbin: Appointment in Sacramento for a fitting.

I stared at his message and studied the words. I had to be missing a secret meaning. Fitting for a tux? I didn't remember him saying anything about a wedding he was in.

My delay made bubbles appear at the bottom of the screen while he typed.

Corbin: Prosthetic. I'm getting one that looks like a wooden peg leg. That way I can dress up for Spirit Week and Halloween next year.

I snorted, and a piece of lettuce caused me to gag and cough.

"You all right there, li'l piggy?"

I swiveled my phone to show her his message, and she laughed. "He's twisted. I like him."

How's poker?

Corbin: Grammy's winning of course. But Aunt Sue bought cupcakes from a store down that road that makes cupcakes. There's caramel inside. CARAMEL!

He sent a picture of himself, pushing the cupcake into his mouth. I could make out Grammy laughing in the background, head thrown back and mouth wide open.

Not fair! I love caramel.

Corbin: As MamaBear says: STBY

———— ⌐ • ┌————

MamaBear dropped me at the curb the next morning, with a promise that she'd pick me up after school. I popped open my handy-dandy umbrella and stomped in every single puddle on the way to Corbin's car.

"Nifty rain boots." He took the umbrella handle and kicked the Mustang door shut. It slammed with a screech and heavy thud.

I flexed my toes in the polka-dotted boots. "Bought 'em last year and never got to wear them." We crossed the wet pavement and were onto the sidewalk when I lurched to a stop, remembering my secret plan to help Marigold with her list. "Oh, I gotta use the library computer at lunch today."

"Okay. Anything wrong with your laptop?"

"No. I keep forgetting to look up Marigold's family information and I think the computer in there has the ancestry thingy."

He swung the door to the hallway open and folded the umbrella down. "The ancestry thingy?"

I shook my head. "I know that's not what it's called, but I'm trying to find out if Marigold has any living relatives left." An abbreviated version of her story and list spilled out before the first bell sounded. "If there is family, I'd like to find them before Christmas as a surprise for her. Maybe set up a video call."

"That's nice of you."

"Don't tell anyone. It would ruin my reputation." I hustled to *Español,* and he ducked into World History.

I scribbled flowers into the margin of my lined paper, unable to make anything more than a daisy. Along the bottom of the paper, a little garden of four flowers blossomed, their leaves revealing the names of Marigold and her sisters. How hard could it be to find a family of flower names from northern California?

In second period, while Mr. Hammond explained the ultra-exciting tax and commerce of the 1950s, I made a pyramid-shaped list of names and places before passing it to Corbin for his thoughts.

"Mom's name? Where is mom from?" His penmanship was one step above hieroglyphs.

I knew I'd forgotten a detail. "Japan" was added to the top of the pyramid next to "Mother." To the side, I added and underlined the word "Camp." There had to be some sort of records for those secret camps that weren't in our history books.

Madison badgered me at the lockers before lunch. "You never sit with me anymore!" She turned her bottom lip down.

"What?" My protein bar hung from my mouth while I shuffled books to my bag. "I sit with you every day."

"Yeah, you and wonder boy." She spun a lock of hair around a magenta-tipped nail. "Where is your bae?"

"He's not my bae." My ears felt like they were on fire.

"Denial is the first step." She needed to shut up before Corbin walked around the corner.

I ripped my zipper closed and straightened. Hopefully the six inches I had on her would be intimidating. "He's my friend. That's it. Nothing is going on between us."

Madison's matte-painted lips parted in a wicked smile. "Down the rabbit hole you go, Alice." She winked and slammed her locker shut. "Gotta go find Josh and tell him the news. Tootles."

"Mads, no."

She was already waving her glossy fingernails over her shoulder without turning around. This was going to go poorly and all sorts of wrong. Frantic, my fingers flew across my phone.

Please don't tell Josh. I swear, nothing is going on.

Mads: JK. U wud tell me, right?

If I didn't answer this, she would assume I was lying about telling the truth.

Yes.

I stalked to the library, grateful Corbin hadn't shown up when she was interrogating me. Mads would've said it in front of him simply to get a reaction from us both. She lived and breathed for drama and Instagram posts.

He was hunched over the computer in the library. "Thought I'd get here early and save a computer for you. I'm already…nine minutes into my fifteen minute allotment." Corbin had an ancestry site pulled up and I saw Marigold's name in the search box.

"Thanks." No need to recount Madison's overactive imagination.

"Coming up empty with Marigold. Thought we could try one of the sisters' names."

I squinted at the screen. "No results. How weird. How about her husband Kenny Williams?"

He typed in the name. "Nada."

"Kenneth?"

"I guess I could expand the approximate date of birth and death." Corbin made the adjustments and the screen was littered with hits.

"That's not going to work. I need to find out her maiden name and her mom's name."

He logged off and stood up. "You going to try and stop by after school?"

"If MamaBear will let me." I sent her my request via text.

"I'll give you a ride to youth group, if you need it."

My brain crashed into reasoning—I was the trusty sidekick in need of transportation. Like Batman and Robin, I rode shotgun or in the motorcycle sidecar. Thank goodness I didn't require a cape or have to wear my underwear outside of my pants. "Let me see what my mom says and I'll let you know."

Like magic, my phone growled.

MamaBear: I can drop you off, then hair appt before church. Can you hang out with her until I'm done?

Yeah. I'll do my homework.

MamaBear: See you at the curb

"Got it covered." I slid my phone into my pocket. "See you later."

"Yup." He loped away, thumb scrolling his phone screen. I'd never noticed that he wore a belt and hoped there wasn't a hideous buckle hidden under his T-shirt.

Homework piled up after each class. My backpack nearly tipped me backwards under my umbrella as I joined the pack of minions waiting for their rides. Deep under the layers of my buttoned-up jacket, my phone growled from my hoodie pocket. I struggled to find it and not drop the umbrella handle.

MamaBear: SWAT call out. Take the bus.

The giant yellow bus number 1986 rumbled by. Great. And her phone would be off or in her car while she scrambled to get to the station. I jogged toward the parking lot, typing a desperate text. I didn't want to walk, no matter how cute my rain boots were.

Are you still at the school?

Corbin: Yeah.

Can I get a ride?

Corbin: Yeah

My side ached, and I slowed to a walk. Of course, the student parking lot was on the opposite side of the campus. As I rounded the last building, the dark blue Mustang was pulling back into his normal spot.

The wipers squealed across the windshield as I slid into the passenger seat. "You didn't need to come back for me."

"Figured something came up since you needed a ride." He eased the shifter into reverse.

"Yeah, Mom got a SWAT call out." I tore my gaze from his long fingers flexed around the gearshift. The sidekick shouldn't stare.

"Sounds exciting."

It was musty in the cab. "Usually isn't. I don't like it when it's exciting, though." My breath fogged up the window. "She's never been hit, but she's been shot at, and that was the worst night of my life. Most people see the news clips and don't pause to think that every officer involved is a mom or dad or kid, but I do."

"Yeah. I feel that way when there are videos of car crashes."

Time to switch paths. "I like kitten videos," I said.

Corbin burst out laughing.

"The best ones are of people letting kittens climb all over them. They are so happy."

"I disagree," he said as he pulled into Willow Springs. "Cat videos that have the meows timed to heavy metal music."

I gathered my backpack and umbrella. "You'll have to show me sometime."

"You need a ride to youth group?"

"I have no idea. Depends on MamaBear."

He held up his index finger. "Don't forget to get Marigold's maiden name."

My face scrunched. "Thanks, Sherlock." I bolted to the entrance and into the building, turning in time to see him leave the parking lot.

"Hey," Jamie barked at me.

I turned. Her platinum hair now sported deep purple tips. "Yeah?"

"I have a whole stack of drawings and letters here." She disappeared behind the desk. A box slapped the desktop before her head reappeared. "There are scarves and hats and stuff in there too."

"Thank you." I hoped there weren't any weird, dirty socks

included. Never know what surprise a person in memory care could slip in, thinking it was a valuable treasure.

Hugging the box to my chest, I made my way to Marigold's room. But not before being stopped by Jasmine.

"You are so beautiful."

I imagined her eyesight was failing, since my hair was stuck to my cheek and everything else was drooping from the rain. "Thank you, Jasmine."

"Oh, you know my name!" She lit up and immediately scowled. "Do I know you?"

"Yes, we've met. I'm Tori."

"You remind me of my goddaughter."

"I gotta go. I'll see you later."

As I passed her wheelchair, she latched onto my jacket. I looked down and her eyes were filled with tears. "I don't want to forget you."

"It's okay." I dropped to my knees. "I'll see you later, okay?"

"Be a good girl and run to the butcher for a ham hock. I'd like to get the soup started before your father comes home."

That was new. "Okay." I straightened and hurried to Marigold's room.

A middle-aged man stood next to her bed. She sat atop the comforter and lifted tiny two-pound weights, alternating each arm into the air. "Good job, Mrs. Williams…I mean, Miss Marigold." Ha! He'd been shamed into submission, too.

I deposited my bag onto the floor and plopped my weary bones into my chair.

"Victoria Grace," Marigold wheezed, pushing a weight above her head. "You are not an elephant."

"My bag was heavy."

"It is better to offer no excuse than a bad one, according to President Washington."

I grumbled, stood up, and then methodically sat. Even with his back to me, I could see the physical therapist grin. Whatever.

"Nicely done. What homework do you have tonight?" She surrendered the weights and grimaced when he lifted her leg from the bed. "Slowly, please." He obeyed.

My laptop powered up. "I have homework in every class."

"That sounds ridiculous. Altogether too much work is given in school."

"Amen," I murmured, pulling out my English book and logging onto the school portal.

"That's all for today, Miss Marigold." He collected the small weights and patted her hand. "Nice workout. I'll see you on Friday."

I didn't want to work on English. I needed information and waited until the therapist left to pounce. "Do you speak Japanese?"

"No. Mother would not allow it."

"That's unfortunate. It's your heritage."

"Mother saw it differently. When she came to the United States with Father, she became an American and worked very hard to learn English. Even when the Yashimotos came over to dinner, they all spoke English. They were very proud to be Americans." She leveled her eyes at me.

But I had to push forward—it would be worth it. "What was your mother's name?"

"Minnie."

"Like Minnie Mouse?"

Marigold swung her small legs from the bed to the floor. "She changed it when she married Father and he brought her home to California, far before Minnie Mouse was ever created." Her eyebrow ticked up a notch. "Minoru Nippon became Minnie Olson."

"Minoru." I tried the foreign name across my tongue. "It's very beautiful."

"It was also very Japanese."

Out of her view, I opened a note in my computer and typed in her mother's names. "You grew up a couple of hours from here, right? Down near Sacramento?"

"You are up to something, Victoria Grace. It will not do." Her courteous words were tainted with suspicion.

"I'm sorry." I wasn't, but maybe she wouldn't be so agitated. "Was trying to be polite and have a conversation."

She grabbed the bed railing and stood. Even at full height, she was barely taller than my head, where I sat. "Do not dig in a garden you are not welcome into. My family is gone. Nothing will change that."

"Okay. I'm sorry. I'll get to work on my English." But I didn't. I punched in her mother's name into a search engine on another tab before returning to my work. Maybe a change of topic would cheer her up. "We were discussing tax and commerce today in History. Made me think about the Hollywood Canteen."

"Plenty of commerce happened there." Marigold shuffled to her armchair and took a seat. "My favorite was when Miss Davis would play the cigarette girl."

"Bette Davis?" I'd done plenty of snooping since our first meeting, and Marigold rubbed elbows with Hollywood's first A-list actors.

"Yes. She and Miss Hayworth were favorites of the soldiers, along with my mistress. Didn't matter the day, you could always bump into a friendly face."

Hobnobbing with the stars. I pulled up images and swiveled my screen to her.

"Yes, there she is!" Marigold started to point, but pulled back her hand before I could stretch and see who she indicated among the screen of black-and-white photos. Dang. Almost found out who her mistress was. "There is Mr. Hope and Miss Temple. They also came to dinner once or twice."

"Who was your favorite?"

"My favorite what, dear?" she asked without diverting her eyes from the images.

"Your favorite person at the Canteen."

A sly smile crossed her dry lips. "My mistress, of course."

"And you won't tell me her name?" My lips pouted. "Ever?"

"You are the one digging for information, Detective Weston. I do believe, one day, you will figure it out."

I groaned and smiled. "You're impossible."

"It's what keeps them guessing, dear."

Fifteen

CORBIN LET ME HAVE THE ARMCHAIR AT YOUTH GROUP later that night. We'd jumped up and down and were shushed when we found Daisy Olson on the library computer the next day. He trapped me in a sidearm hug near the lockers and I froze. Madison twitched her eyebrow. He held the doors open for me and blew up my phone with randomness the rest of the week.

Corbin: Beanbags are great.

Corbin: Today I will be awesome. Or I'll spill food on my shirt and trip over stuff.

Corbin: Penguins are insufficient walkers.

Corbin: If you were the last person on Earth, zombies wouldn't attack you, purely out of respect.

We engaged in cat video wars and compared playlists. Though I was impressed with his variation, I was horrified with the country music he tucked away on a list titled "Lone Star State."

"Aw, come on. You gotta give me a little country for a boy who grew up in the heart of Texas."

I gagged. "No. Never."

"I'll change your mind. There's a country tune out there that'll worm its way into your head." He flicked through the songs then paused. "Can you roll your tongue?" Corbin stuck out his barrel-rolled tongue at me. How perfectly bizarre.

"Of course." I mirrored him.

His chin lifted and I knew there was a challenge coming by his smug grin. "But can you make a *w*?" A pink, lumpy tongue peeked out from above his lips, in the perfect shape of the lowercase letter.

"Holy cow." I twisted and pulled my tongue around. Nothing.

"But wait, there's more!" Corbin made a weird sucking sound and pushed his tongue out between his teeth twice. Then, a bizarre miracle—the next time it appeared, it was neatly folded in half.

"You're a unicorn," I said.

His tongue unfolded and he grinned. "There is nothing rainbow or glitter about my farts."

This boy. His weirdness knew no bounds. It was perfect and made me feel all sorts of stupid.

I split my weekend between work, Willow Springs, church, and never-ending homework. Mr. Bolt bustled around like a gnat in my ear each shift. "Let's hustle. Get going." January. Sweet, sweet January. I could apply for another job and leave the little man far behind. I would miss the free movies, though.

Midway through my Chemistry homework late Sunday night, my phone buzzed. My eyes ached from staring at the laptop screen, I got up from my desk and flopped into bed. I could imagine Marigold's horrified face.

Corbin: Gotta leave by 5 tomorrow morning.

STBY. I'll still be asleep.

Corbin: Hopefully these doctors don't have to start the process all over and can use my other doctor's measurements.

Sorry.

What else was there to say? "Hope they don't hurt your stump?" Even I wasn't that crass.

Corbin: Want to see my leg without my leg?

I didn't even have time to decide before a picture popped up. It wasn't horrific or stomach turning. It seemed...painful. Below his hairy kneecap, the skin was all pink and stretched.

Does it hurt?

Corbin: Sometimes. Not right now. I'm sure after the appts I'll be sore. When you touch it, it feels like beef jerky.

I burst out laughing. I'd never think of beef jerky the same again.

I gotta finish Chem and English but my eyes are burning.

Corbin: Done and done.

Overachiever.

Corbin: G'night

Night.

My phone alarm shocked me into morning. Apparently, I fell asleep after the conversation, and MamaBear covered me with a blanket during the night.

She may have kept me warm, but MamaBear didn't plug in my phone, and I was down to forty percent battery with thirty minutes before breakfast. Thank goodness I had helped myself to Corbin's beanie after church. I crammed it over my unwashed hair and into clean jeans and a camouflage hoodie I'd bought as a dare when MamaBear found it on a clearance rack.

I barely made it to the bus stop on time, with a protein bar hanging out of my mouth. School did not go as planned. History had a substitute teacher, which allowed me to finish my English assignment. Madison was absent with another fatal disease, so I poked around the ancestry site at lunch but came up empty because an impatient freshman kept tapping the corner of his plastic binder during my entire fifteen minutes. Corbin wasn't answering his texts. Everything seemed dull and boring—up until the moment I checked my phone between fifth and sixth period, crossing the grassy patch between buildings.

MamaBear: Sheila called me. Marigold is at the hospital. She is okay. Call me.

And the world faded to white.

———⌐ ∘ ⌐———

"Are you okay?"

My eyelids refused to cooperate and open. They were heavy. Why did I feel like I was waking up after four hours of sleep?

"Hey, hi…Tori?"

And who was this guy calling my name?

Finally, my eyes pried open. It was so bright, and I lay on my back. Said voice came from my right and belonged to Zane. Ah, his muscles strained beneath his shirt and he brushed the hair from my face. Maybe a dream? But I was at school… A slow recognition plodded through my hazy brain: I was on the ground.

I was on the ground?

In a flurry of movement, my arms and legs refusing to cooperate, I struggled to stand.

"You're gonna pass out again," Zane said, pulling me up by my elbows.

"I passed out?" My words barely made it past my slow-moving tongue. I felt dizzy when he held onto each of my shoulders after I was fully upright.

A group of kids massed near my recently collapsed body dispersed. No doubt most of them had taken pictures and videos instead of checking my pulse. I probably was already on the internet. Great.

Zane's eyes bounced back and forth between my own then dipped to my chest and back up again. "Yep. Like a frat girl." His disappointing response caused my stomach to churn. Corbin would never say anything like that.

Although grateful for his help, I declined Zane's assistance and wobbled to the office. The nurse called my mom and exchanged a handful of one-word answers before telling me MamaBear would be there shortly to pick me up. I was glad it was MamaBear's day off and I wouldn't be stuck lying down on the blue vinyl bed until the bus took me home.

I fished out my phone to let her know I was light-headed, but okay. Then, I shot off a message to Corbin.

Don't know much, but Marigold is in the hospital. I'll let you know when I know more. Hope your appointments are going okay.

My mind was in high gear, trying to figure out what could've possibly sent her to the hospital. She seemed fine on Wednesday.

"Hey, wimp." MamaBear took my backpack after she signed me out. "I'm taking you straight to the hospital to see if they will let you visit, okay?"

I nodded, my eyes full of tears.

Having never been to a hospital before, I didn't know what to expect. I trailed after MamaBear to the front desk and then to the elevators. Everywhere, people were talking quietly into phones or tapping their screens. A couple of gurneys passed us in the hallway, and I was freaked out that one might hold my old friend.

We stopped outside a door, and MamaBear nodded for me to go inside. Inside the room, a striped curtain hung from the ceiling, parted a few inches. Marigold's thin frame seemed even smaller in the sterile hospital bed. She was sleeping. My heart ached when I saw the tubes in her nose and the IV in her slim arm, a computer monitor near her head with different lines and numbers.

"This is the infamous Marigold?" MamaBear whispered. Though the two heard much about the other, they'd never met face-to-face.

"It is," Marigold rasped. She opened her eyes and smiled. "You must be the notorious MamaBear."

"Guilty as charged." MamaBear advanced to the bedside. They clasped one another's hands when a doctor-looking-person entered dressed in a pressed white jacket and stethoscope draped around his neck.

"Mrs. Williams, I'm Dr. Trent. Are these ladies family of yours?" Although he spoke, his eyes never left the clipboard in his hands.

"No, they are not." Her low voice caused my body to react; I stepped forward to rub her feet through the blankets.

The doctor flipped papers on a clipboard, mumbled something

about healthcare laws, and asked us to step out while he discussed Marigold's prognosis.

"Young man." Marigold's unexpected, sharp tone made me grin. Oh, he was busted. "You should ask me if I would mind having them in the room while you talk. Had you asked instead of assumed, I would have told you that these are dear friends and I do not mind them hearing what you have to say."

I covered my mouth with my hand to hide my grin and saw MamaBear do the same.

For the first time, the young doctor's eyes lifted from the paperwork. "I apologize, Mrs. Williams. Please forgive me. Sometimes, I get in a hurry with my rounds."

She nodded her acceptance, and Dr. Trent laid out her grim prognosis: congestive heart failure. Due to her age, they would start on the lowest doses of the available medication. He took her vitals while MamaBear and I stood to the side. After he left, the room was silent.

"Well, we always take mortality for granted." Marigold smoothed the blankets, her voice suspiciously upbeat. "I still see myself as a young lady in my mind's eye, but the years have finally caught up with me, I suppose."

"It's not a death sentence," I blurted.

"No, child, but it is coming."

———— • ————

Despite my pleas, both Marigold and MamaBear insisted that I return to school the next day.

"Staring at me with sad eyes won't change a thing, Victoria Grace."

MamaBear dropped me off. I dragged my feet down the halls. Madison provided an embarrassing play-by-play for her female problems via text, since she stayed home again. How that girl passed her classes, I didn't know.

I nearly dropped my phone when it rang as I spun my combination into my locker before the first bell. At least Madison wasn't there to see me smile when I answered Corbin's unexpected call.

"Hey." Casual. I needed to sound unhurried and relaxed, like Dr. John Watson.

He yawned into the phone. "Mornin'. Any news on Marigold?"

"Nope. Only that it's not good." The internet gave me a waterfall of information on congestive heart failure. It was bad. Really, really bad. Her age didn't help either. I even searched for organic and homeopathic remedies, hoping to find the magic bullet.

"Sorry to hear that."

I sighed, wishing I had a bottom locker to kick closed. "And they made me come to school today."

"Your mom and Marigold?" He yawned again.

"A giant conspiracy theory about my grades suffering. You sound tired."

A third yawn filled my ear. "It's a big bucket of disaster here. They have to start all over with their own measurements and will only use my doctor's notes if needed."

"So, poking and prodding?" The first bell rang.

"Yeah. I'm sore."

I loitered in the hall while my classmates filed in. "Only a few appointments today, though?"

"Hopefully getting casted by noon and then we'll be on the road. Home by dinner. Aunt Sue is making pot roast." I could practically hear him drooling.

"Okay, gotta go. I'll text you later."

"Y'all have fun in class today." He chuckled, and the line disconnected.

Between classes, I checked my phone. Finally, between second and third period, an update.

MamaBear: She'll be discharged today. They'll let me know when she's ready and I'll take her to Willow Springs.

Thanks Mom.

MamaBear: Tor, it's not a good situation.

She wasn't being cruel. MamaBear wanted to warn me, give me the facts, and prepare me for the freight train headed in my direction: Marigold wasn't going to survive this. MamaBear was trying to soften the blow the only way she could, without putting me in a bubble of happy-go-lucky fantasy.

I know. Thanks. If you are still at WS when I get out of school, I'll walk over.

In Creative Writing, Mr. Glass droned on about punctuation, the em dash versus the en dash. Did I really need to know this before I graduated? My pen swirled designs in the margin of my notebook. Soon enough, flowers appeared between the lines. Marigold channeled my thoughts through my doodles.

Deep in my hoodie pocket, my phone vibrated. Should I? Mr. Glass clicked the smartboard into life—green light. A born rebel, I pulled the phone from my sweatshirt.

Corbin: You shouldn't check your phone during class.

You shouldn't send me messages.

I leaned forward onto my left hand, elbow resting on the desk. My right hand alternated writing random words and flicking through my phone screen under the desk.

Corbin: How's M?

MamaBear is taking her home later.

After a few seconds, I added a smiley emoji. Maybe it would help me feel better. It didn't. If anything, it made my brain churn through the "what-if's." It was a terrible way to die.

Corbin: What's for lunch?

Didn't even look. Probably leftover spaghetti.

Corbin: My fav. Swap you for my sandwich.

Not a chance if there is mayo involved. And you're 2 hours away.

Corbin: Don't change the subject. It's only eggs and vinegar.

And I'm buying a brand-new Mustang tomorrow. No deal.

Alone for lunch, I found Daisy Olson through the ancestry portal. I pushed my finger against the screen to read the tiny print on the Sacramento County 1940 census. I clicked the link and stared at the looping cursive writing on the census. This was going to take forever, trying to decipher the names.

As my fifteen minute timer sounded, I finally found her name on the left column. She was listed as the daughter of Minnie Olson.

Meh, I already knew that. I clicked back to the original page. Maybe there was something else, and no geek was breathing down my neck this time.

There was another link. It took me to a personal family tree. A few clicks later, and I found her information:

"Daisy Olson Jamison. B: Sacramento, California, 1925. D: Auburn, California, 9/26/1986."

Neatly in a row beneath her name, six of Daisy Olson Jamison's children, twenty grandchildren, and an oversized pack of great-grandchildren.

Daisy had survived and Marigold had a family.

Sixteen

MAMABEAR SENT A TEXT, LETTING ME KNOW THAT SHE had another interview for the K9 position and that I needed to stay with Marigold. God must've had a bit of grace for me because the rain stopped by the time I walked to Willow Springs. The breeze didn't make it a pleasant trip, but I jogged and reasoned that it would help get me into better shape for basketball. And maybe it would pass as an excuse to Coach Neems, since I had absolutely avoided him in the hallway earlier.

I had a page full of scribbled names and dates for Daisy's kids and grandkids because the stingy aide wouldn't let me print the info. "It's not related to any school project," she hissed. "You shouldn't even be using the website if it's not for history." I'm pretty sure she could have been the female version of Kylo Ren, with her severe cut, dyed-black hair, and bossy attitude.

Frightened that she would use the Force to cut my internet feed, I'd nearly run back to the computer. I took a screen shot of the family tree, along with anything else I could open before the aide appeared at my shoulder, signaling the end of my free ride.

I sent the main page picture to Corbin as I maneuvered the crosswalks and uneven sidewalks. He still hadn't let me know how the casting went or if they were on the road.

Found her, like really found her.

Corbin sent me a snap of him in a waiting room, under a clock, his expression undeniably irritated.

Corbin: Was supposed to see the dr. 2 hours ago.

That bites. How's Grammy handling it?

Another picture showed her working needles and yarn in her lap, glasses perched low on her nose.

Corbin: Never learned to crochet, myself. But she is making it for Marigold.

I wanted a grammy like that! MamaBear's mom died when I was seven and I didn't remember much—only the sheepskin covered rocking chair which sat in the corner of our living room. Nana would sit me deep in the pelt and push the chair up and down with her foot.

That's sweet. You going to wrap it and take credit for it?

Corbin: Duh.

I just got to Willow Springs. Marigold is here. Catch ya later.

Jamie barely glanced over the top of her black-rimmed glasses as I passed. And right when I thought I could make it to Marigold's room without interference, Jasmine locked eyes with me. Every day, the same story. But this was a new one, about a fall in the supermarket. Nonstop with her details, I hummed indecisive noises when she paused and looked to me for reassurance.

"Okay." I reached down and patted her hand, knowing I'd never reach Marigold's room before supper at this pace. "I'll see you tomorrow." Jasmine continued to mumble after I waved and walked away.

I recognized the comforter tucked under Marigold's chin—it was the one from the top shelf in our closet. MamaBear pulled it down when I was sick, repeating the story of the material's magical powers to heal when used with chicken noodle soup. I turned back into the hallway, slumped against the wall, letting my tears fall where Marigold couldn't see them. I didn't want her to die. No one believed in me the way that she did, other than MamaBear.

It wasn't fair our time was now going to be measured in days and hours.

Once I'd sniffed my runny nose and wiped the tears with my hands, I stepped back into the room and tiptoed to my chair. After making sure she still slept, I slid my backpack to the floor and pulled out the laptop. As it powered up, I took a picture on my phone of Marigold and sent it to Corbin.

An email was flagged in my inbox. It was from the coordinator of the letter project, and the subject line blared, "You girls are amazing!" My lips pressed my smile tight as I opened the message and then the link inside.

The page loaded up, and my hands flew to cover my mouth. The selfie I'd taken and sent with our application filled the header, larger than I was comfortable with, below the title "Past to Present, for Our Service Personnel."

"What's got you in a dither?" Over the laptop's screen, Marigold's nose wiggled against the clear tubing in her nose.

"Sorry if I woke you, but let me show you." I took the computer to her bed and held it for her to see, then read it to her.

Marigold had tears in the corners of her eyes. "And to think, I was deciding between needle and thread and an apple."

I closed the laptop and knelt on the floor next to her. "I don't understand." Maybe her confusing words were a side effect of the medicine?

"I found myself at a market one afternoon. No one would hire me and I was down to my last dollar and a quarter." Her bony fingers laced together. "Toward the back of the market, a beautiful woman grabbed a can of pork and beans and a jar of applesauce. Even without makeup and her hair tucked into a handkerchief, I knew her from the cinemas.

"I couldn't understand how a movie star would be in a market next to me." Marigold nudged the tubing again. "She was utterly confused, looking from the can to the jar and back to the shelf. Even though she would never admit it, I believe my mistress was offended when I asked if she needed help. She told me if I could make her dinner that very night for less than a dollar, and she liked it, that I was hired."

"That's amazing." I imagined bumping into Anne Hathaway or Halle Berry, walking up and down the aisles of the grocery market on the corner.

Her grin slanted sideways. "My mistress said if she didn't like the meal, I would have a great story for my folks. I made ham and potatoes, with spinach. She had sugar at the house, and I made bananas and cream for dessert."

"So..." I drew out my word, searching for a polite way of asking. "Where did the needle and thread come in?"

"Of course, you younger folk wouldn't consider that." Marigold coughed, and I stood to tweak her pillows. "I had exactly two dresses and one set of hose. My favorite dress had dropped the hem. It was no good trying to find a job appearing shabby."

"And the apple?"

Her thin eyebrows stretched up. "Oh, I could make an apple last for two days. I had exactly enough money to make it one week when I found my mistress with a can of beans."

"Wait a sec." My brain screeched to a stop. "Why were you in the same aisle with her if you were buying a needle and thread and an apple?"

Marigold giggled until she coughed. I filled her water glass and she took a few small sips. "Thank you, Victoria Grace. You caught me. I saw her walk into the store and was so enamored by her presence, that I followed her into the store."

"Oh, you were a stalker!"

"I was not inappropriate. I offered to help her." A cute patch of pink bled into Marigold's cheeks.

My phone buzzed in my pocket.

MamaBear: Another interview. I've texted Sheila and good news! You get a low sodium pot roast dinner.

Gross.

MamaBear: It's good for you.

Yum.I.Can't.Wait.

MamaBear: Shush, you ungrateful brat.

Ha! Corbin and I would both be eating pot roast tonight.

Sheila popped her head into the doorway. "Hello, you two! I thought I heard you in here, Tori." Her hair was twisted into a bun and secured with a ball point pen. "And I made your dinner reservation." She exaggerated her wink. "How's our girl?"

"I am glad to be back home." Marigold extended her hand and clasped Sheila's. "The hospital didn't keep a snack drawer."

"Your canula looks like it's a bit loose. Let me fix that." Sheila fiddled with the nose tube again. She turned and whispered to me, "That's what the plastic tube in her nose is called, in case you didn't know."

Marigold pushed herself more upright. "Oh, you need to see Victoria Grace's computer. There is a clever article about our letters."

I woke up the screen, and Sheila squealed after she was finished. "Can you email this to me? I need to print it out for everyone!"

My cheeks burned. I didn't want the attention. "Uh, sure." I forwarded it to Sheila and hoped she would forget to print it.

"Didn't you send off those letters last week?" Sheila double-checked Marigold and moved toward the door.

"Yeah. My mom shipped them two-day so they could be tracked and wouldn't miss the deadline."

Sheila beamed. "Well, you tell her thank you for me. Such a treat, having volunteers like you two." And off she sped, down the linoleum hall.

"You should get to your homework, young lady." Though she tried to sound stern, Marigold broke into laughter.

"Let me send a text to Corbin first. He was asking how you are."

"Will he be by this week?"

"Probably tomorrow. He's been out of town for doctor's appointments."

Her face pulled together. "Sounds serious. Is he all right?"

I smiled as I pulled out my phone. "Yeah. He has a prosthetic leg and needed to get special measurements for a new one."

"I've never met anyone with a wooden leg before."

I could feel my face betray the awkwardness of her words.

"Oh, that's not the correct term. Does he have a wooden leg?"

My laughter bubbled through in a snort. "He actually has a metal leg." I wished he was here to enjoy our humor at his expense. He'd probably do something absurd, like lapse into a pirate voice.

Ahoy, matey. Marigold called your leg wooden.

Corbin: My leg happened to come up in conversation?

Random, right? She can't wait to get to know you.

Corbin: On the road. Should be getting home right when dinner is ready.

Speaking of food, I also will be enjoying roast of pot.

"Victoria Grace, what are you doing?"

"Sending text messages to Corbin. He's driving back from Sacramento now."

Corbin: You weren't invited. There isn't enough. It's miiiiiiine.

I'm eating at Willow Springs. Don't be jealous.

Marigold sniffed. "That doesn't sound like you're working on homework."

Corbin: Hahahahahahahahahaha. Loser.

I groaned and dug out Chemistry.

Gotta go. She's cracking the whip on homework.

After flying through Chem and English, I stuttered on Algebra. It never made sense. Instead, I reread my texts.

Marigold cleared her throat. "It never ceases to amaze me that your phone is a small computer."

"It also plays music." I started a playlist I worked on the previous night. Marigold's rapturous expression was worth the research as popular tunes from the forties and fifties echoed in her small room.

"Simply delightful!" She sang or hummed to them all as I finished my homework, making math tolerable.

When a nurse whispered into my ear that dinner would be served in fifteen minutes, she made me jump. "I didn't want to wake her."

Marigold had apparently taken a nap while I was buried in Spanish. She was peaceful, bundled up in my magic comforter, mouth slightly open.

I left my phone on, the swing music playing softly, and followed the cattle call toward the dining hall. How did this kind of thing work? I ended up at a table with Warren, with a plate full of dry beef, mashed potatoes, and green salad. If nothing else, at least I had salad, and the dressing wasn't terrible.

Surrounded by strange old people, I regretted leaving my phone behind. I couldn't send SOS texts to MamaBear and Corbin. I'd even be willing to help Madison rather than wait for the banana pudding dessert.

I excused myself to the restroom. Dumb, but handy. To try and burn time, I checked out each mauve colored picture on the wall. But homework wouldn't wait, so I tried my stealthy approach to my chair and saw Marigold staring at me, eyes narrowed.

"I can't sneak in with you watching." I checked for any missed texts. MamaBear would be another hour.

Marigold nudged her canula into her nostrils as she chuckled. "Sleep with one eye open. How was your dinner? I apologize for falling asleep."

"It was okay." I wasn't going to complain about the lack of taste or the ladies who eyeballed me like I was going to steal Warren from the facility.

"What about school? Any cute, new boys?"

My cheeks ignited with heat. "Oh my gosh. I can't believe you said that!"

"I asked—I didn't say. Besides, your blush is simply adorable." Marigold's chapped, pale lips smiled under her bright eyes.

"Yes, lots of boys. None for me." I eased into the recliner, careful not to plop.

"Excellent, dear," she wheezed before her cough propelled me forward to help her sit. "I believe you already have a first-rate candidate."

I tucked the edge of her blanket under her arms. Maybe I did, but I wasn't going to get stuck in Redding by his dimple. Or Mustang. And Texan drawl.

"He's my best friend." My brain laughed and laughed and laughed at the lie.

"Oh, fiddle-dee-dah. He's the cat's meow and you're stuck on him."

Seventeen

NOSE DEEP IN MY HISTORY TEST NOTES, I DIDN'T EVEN acknowledge the knock on the doorframe.

"Heard they were serving pot roast tonight." My head popped up for that accented voice. Dressed in denim, Corbin leaned against the metal casing, grinning.

Cue a stupid grin that I didn't even try to hide. "What are you doing here?" I really didn't care why, though.

"Victoria Grace, how rude." Marigold's bed hummed as the headboard lifted. "Welcome back, young sir."

"Yeah." He advanced to her bedside. "Rude." Corbin offered his hand and attention to a beaming Marigold. "Thought I'd come by and say hello, since I missed our appointment last week."

She blinked and smiled, like a love-struck fangirl. "You are forgiven. Didn't you recently return from traveling?"

Corbin looked to me and I skimmed my book. I wasn't staring. "Dropped off Grammy and thought I'd come and see if Miss Impolite here needed a ride home."

"I'm not impolite!"

"Lower the level of your voice, dear. The nurses will think you are in distress if you continue." Marigold smoothed her hair down, trying to keep her smile hidden.

I scrunched my lips and pointed to Marigold, then Corbin,

wagging my finger between the two of the culprits. "You're both… meanie heads."

Corbin threw up a set of jazz hands. "Ooooh. Meanie heads." He turned back to Marigold. "I'm not sure I can tolerate such verbal abuse."

My history book slapped closed. "I'll show you abuse," I muttered.

"I can see your point, Mr. Dallas. She is fairly impossible."

"Aren't you supposed to be eating dinner?" I had to figure out a way to separate these two or I'd be soon be reduced to a red-faced, bumbling idiot.

"Ate on the way over. How was the pot roast here?"

Both sky blue and chocolate brown sets of eyes waited for my answer. "It…was…a bit dry, but better than canned soup at home. Oh, and hey. Marigold told me about how she stalked her employer in the supermarket."

Marigold gasped. "I did no such thing, Victoria Grace. For shame!" She turned to Corbin once more. "Did she tell you about our article?"

My cheeks scorched northward to my ears. I didn't want anyone else to know.

"Why no, she didn't."

"Show him, Victoria Grace."

Corbin moseyed to the table and crouched near my laptop. He smelled like rain and fresh laundry. I needed to find out what brand of detergent Grammy used. His brown curls, usually hidden in a hat or beanie, tweaked to the side. I flew through my email password and brought up the website.

His lips moved as he silently read through the article. I saw Marigold smile and nod. I could barely stay seated until he finished reading.

"Impressive. Fifty-two letters in two weeks, along with all the other stuff. I feel bad for not helping."

"I've seen your handwriting." Slowly, I edged my hand away

from his. I was Chewbacca and he was the younger version of Han Solo. "And I'm not sure your crafting skills are up to par. Maybe next year, cowboy." Why did I say that? What was wrong with me?

Corbin stood up, but not before I noticed the blush in his cheeks. "You have no idea about my mad crafting skills."

Not one to back down, I took the bait. "Really? You an avid scrapbooker?"

"Nope."

"Knit a doily in sixty seconds flat?"

He crossed his arms. "Nope."

"Stay inside the lines in a coloring book?"

Even Marigold chuckled at that one.

"Only if I really, really try. I doubt you can figure it out. But I can show you. Hand me a piece of paper."

Marigold stretched her neck back and forth when he sat down across from me in her armchair at the table, paper in hand. I sent MamaBear a text to let her know Corbin would take me home.

"When you're stuck in a hospital and twelve years old, there's not much to do. The video games get boring and coloring books don't cut it." He glanced up from the paper to me for half a second.

MamaBear: How perfectly convenient of your "friend"

Gratefully, Corbin turned back to folding his project. I could feel my blush crawl from my neck to my cheeks.

Will everyone stop saying that?!

MamaBear: But you say he's just a friend, but you say he's just a friend...

At least she just posted a music note emoji and didn't send me a link to the song.

Ma! STAHP!

"Oh, that's origami." Marigold clapped her hands together.

Corbin smiled but kept his head down, tearing carefully down a crease. "Yup. I could make them and have the nurses give them to the other kids. Even the ones in the burn unit."

"Isn't origami Japanese?" I studied Marigold, whose eyes snapped to mine. "It's okay, he knows."

"It is." Corbin still hadn't looked up. I saw the corner of Marigold's pursed lips turn up.

A lightning bolt of inspiration hit and I couldn't help but grin, because I was totally going to amaze her. "*Konichiwa.*"

Unimpressed, she turned her head toward Corbin.

Mental face palm.

I shut my laptop to watch his hands smooth and fold the paper with his big ol' knuckles and gnawed fingernails. The paper was a crumpled mess until, suddenly, it was a paper boat. He pushed it over the lace tablecloth to me. "Haven't made anything in a while, so I thought I'd go with something simple."

"What else can you make?" I flipped the boat over one way and then the next before getting up and handing it to Marigold.

"Uh, a bunch of different kinds of stars, a frog, crane, stuff like that." He sat back in Marigold's armchair, completely filling it top to bottom and side to side. "I used to be able to make Star Wars stuff like X-wings and tie-fighters too."

"What? You have a super-folding power and didn't tell me?" I thrust another piece of paper at him.

Corbin laughed. "I gotta practice and look up the directions."

"You must've been in the hospital quite some time to acquire such skill." Marigold extended the boat back to its maker.

"Yeah." His voice faded. "The first couple of surgeries weren't successful. I was there longer than they anticipated. Origami helped me focus and pass the time."

My stomach flip-flopped. "Longer than anticipated?" How long had he been stuck there? "Did you have to do your school work there?"

"Yup." Corbin pushed the boat back to me, his eyes stuck on the paper. "Heaven forbid a kid try to deal with losing his family and his leg. The psychologist told Grammy it would help get me back to a normal life."

"Pish posh." We both turned and watched Marigold rearrange the edge of the comforter. "Some doctors feel like God Almighty with their opinions." I couldn't tell if she was talking about Corbin's psychologist or Dr. Trent.

"Grammy did more to help me than the shrink. She took me home to recoup. Doctors were ticked. But she hired a nurse and I only went back when it was time to get fitted for a prosthetic."

"Those are expensive, right?" I didn't want my limited knowledge of the subject to shine brightly.

"Crazy expensive. That's why I want to become a computer programmer. There are organizations that build prosthetics out of 3D printers, so it's more affordable. A bunch of geek programmers even make ones that look like dragon scales or superhero armor."

"It's very noble of you to give back." Marigold nudged her legs to the side of the bed. "Now I must ask if you'd be a gentleman and help me into my house shoes."

Corbin retrieved the lavender velour slippers and slid them on, past the yellowed nails and bulging blue veins. "Ma'am." He held her by the elbows as she stood.

"Victoria Grace, I'm afraid my company will be of little use tonight." Marigold tilted her head back and gazed at Corbin, who smiled back. "Let this young man take you home so you can go to bed at a decent hour."

I stuffed my books and laptop into my backpack. Before I pulled the heavy bag to my shoulder, I took a few steps and collected her into a gentle hug. The top of her head was even with my shoulders, and my chin rested on top of her hair when she wound her arms around my waist. Poking into my ribcage, her elbows squeezed tightly. I didn't want to let go, especially when tears pooled in my eyes. One less day with Marigold after I walked out of her room.

She pulled back and took my face in both of her knobby hands. "I'll see you tomorrow." Short white eyelashes batted her tears back.

"Yup." It was the only word that came to mind. I turned to

Corbin and saw my backpack perched high on his shoulder. "Let's jet."

He motioned for me to walk ahead to the door. "Goodnight, Miss Marigold."

"Goodnight, my brave man. See her safely home."

"Yes, ma'am."

Marigold shuffled tiny steps toward the bathroom. "Off with you two." She waved us off with a hand and we left.

After he held the front door for me, I fell into step next to him, down the wheelchair ramp. "Thanks for picking me up. MamaBear's K9 interviews ran late."

"When will she find out if she gets the position?" He went to the passenger side, unlocked the Mustang, and opened the door.

"I'm not sure." I reached across to unlock his door.

Corbin popped the trunk, deposited my backpack, and then slid into the driver's seat. Although he jammed the keys into the ignition, he didn't start the engine. He rubbed his face with both hands and groaned.

"You okay?" Totally something Samwise would say to Frodo. But I didn't have hairy, oversized feet.

"I'm tired. Shouldn't be though. Grammy drove." He rolled his head back and forth on his shoulders.

"Here, turn around." I flailed my hands in a circle until he turned his back to me. "MamaBear says I'm good at rolder shubs."

"At what?"

"Ah. Dyslexia of the lips. Shoulder rubs. You gotta, like, take off that gigantic parka first."

Corbin shucked the fleece-lined denim jacket and tossed it to the back seat. The second my thumbs dug into his taunt muscles, he tensed and held his breath. I hesitated. Would Patrick Star rub SpongeBob's shoulders? He might, if SpongeBob needed it.

I backed off the pressure and worked small circles, staying away from the slice of flesh peeking between his long curls and collar. The patch of skin captivated my attention.

"Yeah, I'd agree with your mom on this one."

My fingers stopped. I switched to a short chopping motion. "After a long shift, it helps her relax. Especially the ones that she doesn't want to talk about."

"I can't imagine what she sees."

The parking lot lights looked mysterious as the windows started to fog over. "It's not only what she sees. Sometimes it's the smell that gets to her, or the fact that she has to go back to the same house over and over and over." I slapped my hands on his shoulders to signal the end of the massage.

"Thanks." He pulled his jacket back on and draped his body onto the steering wheel. "I hope she gets the job."

"Me too. She's put it off for years, while I was younger." My hands were cold without the friction, and I put them under my legs, ignoring the pain when the split vinyl scratched my fingers.

He noticed. "Sorry." The engine rolled over and Corbin turned the heat on full blast. "You'll have to get my defroster from the glove box."

I opened the glove box and found a small towel. "This?"

"The best 1970 has to offer." He mopped the condensation from the windshield, then his window, before handing it back to me. "Did you find out anything else about Daisy's family?"

"Nope." I swiped my window clean and put the cloth away. "I didn't want to be late for Lit." My phone screen came to life, and I pulled up the pictures. "It's weird she had six kids, like their mom did."

Over the idling engine, heavy raindrops plunked the roof and windshield.

"Did you get the contact info to the person who posted the family tree?" Corbin pushed the front vent in my direction.

"I knew I forgot something."

"We can get it tomorrow."

I didn't miss his wording: "we," like him *and* me. I hoped he missed when I cleared my throat. "If the same chick that was there today sees me, she will hover, and you might have to run covert ops all by yourself. I'll have lunch with Madison, all by myself, like old times."

"Sounds like you question the librarian's authority." Corbin slid the car into reverse.

My forehead wrinkled. "I'm not anti-authority. There's a whole lotta people in authority who aren't competent. Besides, her hair is emo and repulsive."

"Judging in your judge hole." He pulled to the street and stopped. "But you're going to have to give me directions, since I don't know where you live."

I called out the turns on the way to the apartment. We were nearly there when my phone growled.

MamaBear: You out gallivanting while unchaperoned?
Nearly home. ETA 2
MamaBear: See you soon.

"You drive without music." The lack of noise, other than the whining windshield wipers, was odd to me.

"The radio broke last year, and I haven't pulled it out to see what's wrong." He thumped on the knobs with his fingers. "Got busy with the move and all."

"But you aren't going to replace it, right?" I waited until he grabbed the steering wheel again to twist the black-and-silver dial. "I mean, it's original to the car."

"Of course. I'm used to it by now, though."

"Lucky me, I don't have to listen to your yee-haw playlist."

Corbin turned into the apartments and parked in a visitor's space a few spots down from our door. He kept the engine running. "I'd never grace your uncultured eardrums with classic country music."

"I know you have those cowboy boots tucked away."

"If I did, it'd be in the trunk, touching your backpack and spreading country through osmosis."

My chin went up. "Your use of the English language is astounding. I commend you, sir." I gave him a slow golf clap.

"Origami and reading. Grammy used to bring me books. Even audio books, when I was being a pain. She stuck to the classics and sprinkled in a few animal warrior stories."

I bounced on the seat. "I read all of those too!"

"Not sure if I read them all, but I have a firm grip on the clan statuses."

My phone growled deep in my pocket.

MamaBear: I hear his car. Don't make me open the curtains.

"My mom is literally the worst." I unsnapped my lap belt and reached for the door handle.

Corbin scrambled to cut the ignition. By the time he'd run around to my side of the car, I was out and closing the door. He kinda seemed depressed, from what I could see in the amber street light, that I hadn't let him open the door.

"I can get my door," I said. No one had ever opened car doors for me, except the time I broke my arm in fifth grade.

"I know, but I don't mind." He sulked to the trunk and retrieved my backpack.

Mental note, let the boy open my door—sometimes. "We're in number 16." I shielded my eyes from the rain.

Corbin walked next to me to the steps. He handed over my bag. "Want a ride tomorrow morning?"

"Let me check with my mom. I'll send you a text." My mother was behind that door, I already knew it.

"Alrighty." He turned to walk away, then stopped and turned back to me. Maybe he needed the address to find the way from his house. "Never mind." Corbin aimed back to his car.

He took a few steps before I raised my voice. "Hey!" Again, he reversed his retreat but stood on the wet asphalt, while I remained on the steps. "I'm basically a girl with the personality of a dude. I don't do well with half sentences or thoughts. Speak your mind, Lone Ranger."

His hair got darker with each raindrop, and he looked miserable, hands mashed into the front pockets of his jeans. At that moment, I didn't mind if he grabbed me and kissed my face off, like a campy, lovey-dovey movie.

Corbin cleared his throat. "I like you. You make me laugh. You're weird. And I wish I had something better to say."

"No," I whispered. "That was pretty good." In cliché romantic style, my heart raced, pitter-pattered, and fluttered.

"Okay." He stayed at the edge of the parking lot. "Well, goodnight, then." Seemed he would play the white knight and wait until I was safely inside.

"Night." I twisted the door handle and abandoned the sidekick status on the steps outside. I sent him a text asking for a ride before the sounds of his engine left the parking lot and floated to my bedroom.

Eighteen

WHAT DOES ONE WEAR THE MORNING AFTER A declaration of like? Obviously, it was a lower status than the four-letter, super-serious word, but it was more than partner-in-crime and required a bit more planning the next morning. Up early for a shower? Check. Breakfast so my stomach didn't speak whale? Check. Teeth brushed *and* flossed. Win.

MamaBear knocked around the kitchen. "Want a ride this morning?"

Keeping annoying mother and her questions away? Not gonna happen. Ever.

I pulled off my red flannel and tried on a blue sweater. Everything looked stupid. "No. Corbin will be here in ten minutes." I settled on the army green zip up jacket. It looked best with my black jeans and lace up boots.

MamaBear appeared in my room, hands on hips. "When was this decided?"

"Last night, after he dropped me off." No lip gloss. Too obvious.

"And you were going to tell me when?"

I exhaled. She always made things difficult when they were simple. "I forgot. Sorry." I squeezed past her to go to the bathroom to swipe on my mascara. Did I really have this many freckles?

"Your lunch is on the counter."

"Thanks." I nearly forgot my deodorant and was lifting my shirt up when there was a knock on the door.

Oh no. No, no, no, no, no. She was going to interrogate him and I was stuck with half an armpit worth of deodorant. If it was anything like the night before, when I finally blurted out that he said he liked me to make her stop, it would be bad. I swabbed the deodorant as quickly as I could while they spoke down the hallway.

"Good morning, Corbin."

"Mrs. Weston."

"I'm not that old. Just Kacey."

"And I'm not that brave, ma'am."

They both stood inside the door when I hurried out, pulling my backpack onto my shoulder. He held his ball cap in both hands.

"Gotta get my lunch." I ducked into the kitchen.

"You dropping her off at Marigold's after school?"

I growled under my breath. She would wiggle the details from him, one bit at a time. I'd danced that dance.

"Yes, ma'am. I can do that." He sounded unsure before I rounded the corner. Corbin smiled at me, and his dimple appeared. "You ready?"

"PB and J for my lunch date with Madison." Out of the corner of my eye, I could see MamaBear sizing me up. She'd practically left me alone the night before and now wanted the details. Nothing would cross my lips. "See ya."

My umbrella opened up after I clicked the button. I held it high for Corbin to walk under. Our fingers brushed when he took the handle from me. Was I supposed to try and hold his hand while he held the umbrella? Did I match his pace or try to graze our arms? And why was I acting like a weird dork who might implode? There wasn't a manual on this junk, and I shifted from one foot to the other while he opened the passenger door.

"Thanks."

He smiled again. "Yup." Bonus.

Balanced on the drive train tunnel, a little speaker caught my attention. "What's that?"

Corbin turned the engine over and messed with his phone. The speaker crooned country music.

"Ah! My ears are bleeding." When I looked at him, he was staring, the corner of his eyes wrinkled with his smile. I turned back to the speaker.

He changed the music. As we drove the back streets to Butte, it felt like there was a bubble riding between us, invisible and making us mute. But at least there was music to fill the silence. I wasn't sure what to ask—if he really meant what he said the night before or what he brought for lunch.

As soon as he pulled into the parking spot, I had to speak. "I'm going to get my own door."

"Okay."

I needed to send a text real quick before Madison caught wind of it and made me feel even more bonkers than I already did.

Mads, he likes me. Don't say anything. Act normal.

Maybe I'd get lucky and she was still home with a fever. I swung my backpack on and put my hands deep into my jacket, only to yank out my phone again when it buzzed.

She filled three lines with hearts and smiley faces. I tucked the phone away before he could see the screen. This was going to be interesting at the lockers with Li'l-Miss-in-Your-Business.

Corbin held up my umbrella and waited for me at the back of the Mustang. I'm relatively certain that his lopsided grin was for me. It made my stomach gooey, my brain flatline, and my lips curve into a smile. I was weird and he liked me.

"You want to catch dinner before church?" He gazed straight ahead, navigating the collection of kids running without umbrellas.

"Sure." Not like my calendar was full or that I wanted dinner at Willow Springs again. The pot roast still sat in my belly like molten lead.

"What do ya want?" He pulled open the door and closed the umbrella. Madison would pounce us in ten seconds flat.

"Tacos. We usually have them on Tuesday but my choices were limited last night," I said, scanning for the mass of blonde curls. She was going to blow this to epic proportions.

He sent a text message. "Grammy makes the best tacos."

"Oh, I thought we were hitting up the drive-thru on the way to church."

Corbin snarled his lips. "Gross. I had enough fast food to last me my whole life."

"Probably hospital food, too?"

He bumped his elbow into mine. "It's not half as bad as drive-thru."

Madison watched our approach in the mirror inside her locker door. "Hey, guys." She spread another coat of red lipstick while I spun my combo in. "I think I lost seven pounds in the past two days. It was brutal."

"Did you have the flu?" I caught her stare in the reflection and silently begged her to remain calm. A squeal escaped me when Corbin dropped down to my eye level and smiled at her in the mirror.

She closed her locker and turned to face us as Corbin straightened and leaned into the lockers behind me. "I'd say it was food poisoning, since my stepmom cooked chicken. I can't believe my dad married the only chick who can't cook. What's that called, when a guy who owns restaurants marries a woman who can't boil an egg?"

"Irony," Corbin said and nudged my boot.

Madison's eyebrow lifted a fraction, then she tossed her hair. "Gotta go get my homework assignments. See you guys at lunch?"

"Just me." I finally turned to look at him. "He's got a project and has to use the computer in the library." I could dive into that dimple.

"Sweet. We can split my lunch. Tootles." With a shake of her French-tipped nails, she sauntered down the hall.

I stashed half of my books and slammed the door. "Ready?"

"Yup." His wide fingers spread across the small of my back as we walked. I took a half step closer to him. He dropped his hand when we arrived at his classroom and the bell vibrated my eardrums. "See you in History."

My stare dropped from those tempting lips to the linoleum tile. If I looked any longer, I didn't trust my actions. Instead, I prodded his Converse with my boots. My cheeks felt like they were going to burst into flames. Why was this so bizarre?

"You're going to be late," he said.

Kids around me scurried in all directions. "Gah!" I bolted toward Spanish. "Bye," I called over my shoulder.

Totally unprepared for the pop quiz in first period, I drifted like a limp balloon to History until I turned the corner and saw Corbin waiting for me at the door.

"Hey." He shoved his phone into his back pocket.

"Hi." What pop quiz? I'd ask for extra credit.

We moseyed to our desks. I kept my head down, the longer side of my hair blocking my view of Corbin, mostly because I wanted to stare and smile, like a dork. But a few times, I peeked over and he grinned back, pen bouncing like a hyperactive Jack Russell between his fingers.

Corbin gathered his books as the bell rang. "I need the rest of Daisy's stuff."

I sent the other pictures as we walked to our next classes. He grabbed my elbow to steer me around a pack of guys I recognized as football players practically blocking the hallway. But he didn't let go until we stopped at the staircase. My Creative Writing class was upstairs and his Geometry was down. We wouldn't see each other unless he was bumped off of the computer since he was going straight to look up contact info for Daisy's family tree after the next period.

"Have fun in the library. Say hi to the mistress of the dark side."

He squeezed his eyes closed and shook his head. "I'll let you know if I find anything."

"Sounds good." I took the stairs two at a time without glancing back.

At lunch, Madison waved me over to the table as soon as I made it through the door. "Spill it." She pushed a cupcake at me.

"Nice to see you too." I shoved the entire thing into my mouth.

"You're disgusting." She tore off a corner of her turkey croissant sandwich and chewed on the dainty bite.

I choked down the last bit with a gulp of water from my lunch. "I am. But I'm also weird and he said he likes me."

"Wait, he likes that you're weird or likes you?"

"Both." I bit off a hunk of PB and J.

Josh slid up to Madison's side. "Hey, babe."

She turned up her nose and stared the other way, sipping from her sparkling water. "Don't you 'hey babe' me. You didn't even call to see how I was."

"I texted you." He groped her stomach and pushed his fingers between the buttons on her shirt.

"You should've called. I wanted to hear your voice."

Ew. I didn't want to deal with this drama tornado without Corbin. I checked my phone.

Find anything yet?

Corbin: Taking pics of the family info when Mistress Vader isn't looking. You weren't joking.

Does it have their mom's name or info?

Bubbles bounced while he typed. I glanced up in time for Mads and Josh to lock lips. I'd never be that gross around other people.

Maybe.

Corbin: Only this:

I zoomed in on the picture he sent. "Minnie Olson, B: Japan. D: 1/1943, Owens Valley Reception Center."

"Gotta go," I announced to the pair across the table.

Madison grabbed my hand. "You owe me an explanation."

I nodded to Josh, who was sniffing her neck. "Not the appropriate time." Hopping over the bench, I grabbed my stuff and headed toward the library. Hopefully, she'd get lost in Josh's face and forget all about me and Corbin.

Corbin: And I've been caught.

I saw his tall frame coming toward me down the hallway. Staring at his phone while still typing, he didn't see me trying to be coy and step into his path. Suddenly, we were a jumble of arms and legs, thrashing to keep upright. I had my nose near his ribcage and felt one giant hand wrapped around my waist while being pulled sideways. When the movement stopped, I was pressed tight against his chest and his other hand was latched onto a nearby locker to steady our bodies.

Mmmm, hugging.

"Unfortunately, I'm going to have to let go of you." My cheek vibrated when he spoke. "My magic leg has shifted and I'm afraid if you don't stand up, we'll end up on the ground."

My feet found solid ground. "I'm sorry!"

"It's okay." Once I was upright, his hand went from my waist to my shoulder and he leaned onto me. "I think I must've knocked the release button."

I panicked. "What do you want me to do? Can I do something?"

He laid his forehead onto mine. "It's fine. It happens. Nature of the prosthetic-bound. Weird things happen. Like you." He rubbed his thumb against my shoulder.

"You're flirting and your leg is falling off. Not that I mind. But shouldn't you sit down?"

"Yeah." He twisted until his back was against the lockers and sank to the ground. "Much better." I squatted next to Corbin as he probed his thigh through his jeans. He shoved, pulled, and then I heard a *click*. "There it is. Never had this happen before." The bottom hem of his jeans crept up, revealing the metal socket. He let out a slow, measured breath, then readjusted his ball cap.

"Magic leg, huh?" I tugged down the bottom of his jeans, to keep any rubberneckers from gawking.

"Grammy came up with it when I got my first leg." Corbin bent his human leg and held out his hand to me. "Give a gimp a hand up?"

I stood and leaned backwards to pull up his lanky frame. He rotated and moved his left leg. Maybe he was testing to make sure it didn't come unlatched again?

"Good to go." Still, he held onto both of my hands, making my brain rubbery and the spot behind my ribcage thrum. And the moment I thought he might lean in to kiss me, the bell sounded. Worst timing ever.

"You sure you're okay?" I retrieved my backpack and his phone, which had landed a few lockers down on the floor.

Corbin took a couple of steps. "Right as rain, as Grammy says. Thanks." He pocketed his phone. "I'll send you the pics I grabbed. That librarian is Satan reincarnate."

My snort was anything but cute. "She's too emo for Satan." I paused at the staircase. "Sorry I made you fall."

"Quit apologizing. It happened. I lost a leg."

I laughed. "Better get a move on, limpy. Wouldn't want you to use it as an excuse for a tardy."

He shuffled away and glimpsed back. That smile again.

Yeah. That was for me.

Nineteen

I'M NOT GONNA LIE. I COULDN'T WAIT FOR SCHOOL TO get out so I could walk around the corner to my locker. Now, I could openly admire the flannel-and-blue-jean-clad boy waiting for me. He was staring at his phone, thumb scrolling the screen, one leg crossed in front of the other. He pushed the bill of his cap up, and his eyebrows dropped. This didn't look good.

"Hey." I bumped his elbow away from my lock and was rewarded with a dimpled smile. "How's the leg?"

"Good. Grammy says dinner will be ready around six." He pulled my backpack from my shoulder and hitched it high on his own. "Can you eat that fast? We only live about seven minutes from church."

"MamaBear calls me a vacuum." I slammed the locker closed.

His hand caught my elbow and nudged me toward the door. "Good to know. You'd be handy in a pie eating contest."

Rain pounded the sidewalk. Yet another day I was thankful I carried my umbrella. "Does anyone still have pie eating contests?"

"Yeah." Corbin raised his voice over the noise of the downpour. "Every summer they have them at our county fair."

"The county fair in Texas?" It would've been downright cozy, pressed into Corbin's side under the umbrella, if it weren't for kids shrieking as they ran by us, soaking wet.

He dodged a girl who stopped in the middle of the sidewalk to stare at her phone. Leaving the umbrella in my hand, he rejoined me after he walked around her. "That was close." Flecks of rain from his sleeve hit my cheek. "Yeah, in Texas—at least in the county I grew up in."

I let him open the door for me. Maybe he'd lean in and—nope. Corbin took a step back and closed the door. Okay. He must be a traditional kind of guy, slow and steady. I could do slow and steady. Heck, I'd done nonexistent up to the day before.

Grabbing my gum out of my jacket, I debated whether to offer him a piece. Would he think I thought his breath smelled? I dropped the pack onto the floorboards after he started the car. "Want a piece?" Smooth.

Corbin pulled a stick of gum out. "*Gracias, señorita.*"

"*De nada*, dude."

Marigold wore a set of white headphones when we arrived, eyes closed and humming a melody. Underneath my comforter, her feet slid back and forth in perfect rhythm. I stopped in the doorway to take a picture. It was a keeper, and I sent it to MamaBear.

We crept to the table and unloaded our homework. Our feet rested against one another's under the table, like we'd always done it. Slow and steady. I was well into Chemistry before Marigold gasped. Our heads swiveled toward her.

"Oh, applesauce!" She pulled the headphones off, and they thumped into her lap. "You gave me a scare."

Marigold folded over with a series of coughs. Corbin moved to help her sit, and I got a glass of water. She drank greedy sips and sucked in deep breaths. When her breathing slowed and she sighed, I took the cup from her hands and set it on the nightstand. My hands were shaking. I curled my fingers into fists to make them stop. She didn't need me to be a wimp.

"Thank you both," she whispered, pushing the canula back into her nostrils.

"Let me get that." Corbin reached around the back of her head and tightened the tubing.

I touched the tablet on her lap. "This is new."

"Yes, I had Sheila help me order it and put music onto it." Marigold tapped the screen to life. She tugged the headphone cord out, and a swing tune blasted through the tiny speaker. "Oh, that's a bit loud."

Corbin lowered the volume. "The Andrews Sisters."

"Indeed. I had the pleasure of knowing their company."

"Really?" Corbin's voice pitched up—he was star struck. He backed up and sat on the arm of the lounger.

"Certainly. They played at the Canteen and also came over a few times. LaVerne was swell, real easy to get along with."

I had no idea who LaVerne was, and my Chemistry wasn't going to get done by itself, so I moved back to my laptop. The two continued to yammer on about dancing and other stuff. I had to concentrate on the temperature conversions for the test on Friday.

Corbin dropped from the arm and into the seat itself. Whatever, dirty plopper. Marigold was busy putting the cord back into the jack and didn't see his infraction. I almost said something until his foot slid next to mine and our calves touched. I smiled into my textbook.

We worked in relative silence until Corbin's phone dinged. He looked at the screen. "Supper time."

After we said goodbye to Marigold, I made sure to slow down in the parking lot so he could open my door. The rain had let up to a sprinkle. I tried to pay close attention to the street names he drove down to remember the directions, in case I ever got a car.

Grammy greeted us at the door. A wave of spices pushed out of the open door, and my stomach rumbled. "Oh, somebody's hungry. Y'all come inside and sit down at the table. Corbie, wipe your shoes."

I mimicked his actions, minus the eye roll. We hung our jackets on the pegs near the door. The red-and-white-checkered dining room was covered with a tablecloth circa 1950s. White cloth napkins folded into triangles were under each of the four forks, matching knives and spoons on the right side of the scalloped-edged plates. Cheese, tomatoes, lettuce, and sour cream were all divvied into fancy bowls. Only the hot sauce was in its original container. I bet she didn't have leftover packets of mild or extra hot sauce in a kitchen drawer, either.

Corbin pulled out a chair for me. I fiddled with moving my chair forward until Grammy reappeared with a plate full of taco shells filled with meat that looked like it could feed twenty or more, followed by a silent woman. Grammy's shadow wore thick glasses, and her white hair was cut so short that it was almost nonexistent. Aunt Sue sat opposite of me after introducing herself.

"Corbie, will you say grace?" Grammy clasped her hands together and bowed her head. And so did I, until Corbin said his "Amen."

Grammy asked how our days went. I answered between bites, trying not to shovel my mouth too full.

"Our flight is on Saturday, Corbie. Remember to get your laundry done."

"What flight?" My taco meat nearly tumbled out through my words, and Corbin's mouth was fuller than mine.

"Headed down to the ranch for Thanksgiving," Grammy said.

My eyebrows rose, and I peered at Corbin. Thanks for the warning, bud.

He wiped the corners of his mouth. "Uncle Richard made us promise to come down for Thanksgiving this year."

Poor me. Separated from the guy I like. Really, *really* like. "When are you guys coming back?" I asked.

Corbin shrugged his shoulders and glanced at Grammy.

"The Saturday after Thanksgiving. We'll stay long enough to help him put the lights up on the house and the big tree out front."

Oh no. They were one of those types of decorating people, with trees for every room. "We're lucky if we remember to get a tree put up a week ahead of Christmas."

"No, these are the lights for the outdoor trees and outside on the main house and barn. It takes a few days with the bucket truck and wiring." Grammy's eyes sparked like the lights she described. "The tree in the house won't go up until after the first Saturday in December, along with the trimmings."

I took a drink of water. "You'll have to take pictures. It takes me fifteen minutes to tape the lights in our front window."

"But Corbie tells me you and your mama are going to start looking at houses soon?"

Did he have evening chats with Grammy? "Hopefully the first week in December." The thought made me giddy. We wouldn't be able to move until after Christmas, but it would be fun trotting around with MamaBear, scoping out neighborhoods. Maybe we'd find one with a pool.

"That's very exciting. Could you pass the cheese?"

I handed her the bowl. "It'll be the first house I've lived in." My phone growled, and I scrambled to snatch it from my pocket. "I'm sorry, I forgot to turn it to silent."

Aunt Sue and Grammy both smiled through their tacos.

MamaBear: Need me to bring you dinner?

At Grammy's. Taco Wednesday. Because Taco Tuesday was absent.

MamaBear: You have betrayed me.

"Sorry, it's my mom making sure I have food." I put down my phone, and no one was eating. I thrust the last bite of taco in my mouth.

"Let's get this cleaned up before church." Grammy gathered her plate and offered to take Aunt Sue's. "You want to come with us tonight, Sue?"

"Not tonight, Rosie." Her answer gave me the distinct feeling that she never said yes.

Aunt Sue retreated down the hallway. I helped shuttle dishes from the table to the kitchen. Grammy emptied and scraped while Corbin filled the sink with soapy water. His sleeves were pushed up to the elbows, and he furiously washed. Grammy switched to rinsing, leaving me clueless.

"Can I help?"

"No, no." Grammy stacked plates into the drying rack next to the sink. "We'll be done here in a jiffy."

I pulled out my phone. "Could I have the password to your Wi-Fi? I'd like to see if I can find any more information on the camp Daisy and Marigold's mom was in."

Corbin's cheeks were pink when he turned, hands still in the suds. "It's 'puppy love,' all lower case, with no space in the middle."

"I never guessed you for that type of password." My phone connected, and I clicked on the first site.

"It's Aunt Sue's. She didn't want me to change it."

"Likely story, big guy."

He chuckled, moving dishes from the soapy water and rinsing them off. Grammy's grin stretched wrinkles into her cheeks.

I bounced from site to site, searching for lists of people who possibly died at the camp. Nothing. The pictures caught my eyes: tiny houses made with lumber and black paper, snow, and long lines of people waiting for food. It was wretched.

By the time I looked back up, Grammy had disappeared and Corbin was rinsing the sink. He glanced over his shoulder at me. "You find anything useful?"

"Nope." I stepped over to the sink. Slow and steady. I started to pull down his sleeve and he yanked away. "Oh, okay. Sorry."

"It's...I don't like..." Corbin slapped both hands on the sink and I jumped.

"It's okay, you don't have to tell me whatever it is." Unless he was a serial murderer and I'd just triggered some kind of killer instinct.

He moved his hand across the counter, toward my elbow, but stopped shy of touching me. "You probably think my arm is horrible."

"I don't know what you're talking about." Of course, as the words tumbled from my lips, my eyes peeked at his bare arm.

A jagged scar snaked from his wrist and ended somewhere under his sleeve. The skin was several variations of pink, stretched and shiny. "It was broken and burned in the accident." He tugged the sleeve down. "I don't…like…"

"What?" He didn't like me. He didn't like anyone seeing his arm. "You gotta tell me before my brain explodes."

Corbin laughed. "Overactive imagination?"

"You have no idea. I can go from zero to one-twenty with two words."

He wiped the counter with a dishcloth and then folded it. His hands stayed busy until he paused and pinched the bridge of his nose, eyes fixed on the window over the sink. "I have issues about people touching me after the accident. My body is a patched-up mess. And I can be a mental basket case with certain sounds and smells."

Of course. How could I not have realized this? But his formerly charred arm didn't matter to me. And I would show him. "That's right up my alley. I'm the weird one, you know." I pushed my hands into my pockets. I probably gave him a heart attack when we fell earlier, all smashed together. Idiot.

The corner of his mouth curled into a smile. "We're gonna be late. Grammy has already walked by twice."

I checked my phone. Crickey. MamaBear would be prowling the door, counting headlights.

We piled into the Mustang, and I happily volunteered for the backseat. The springs were still bouncy, and I bobbed up and down. The only downside was the lack of leg room. I was practically kissing my kneecaps.

Although she tried to appear ordinary, MamaBear hung out near the doors with Bob the usher and casually watched the cars as they pulled in. Once she saw Corbin's, she headed inside, with a nod to Bob.

I was mugged by Jack and Zach as Michelle Branch asked me to babysit a few days during the school break. I readily agreed, seeing as I had no one to hang out with, other than Marigold and MamaBear. Madison would probably head to the Bay Area to her grandpa's, leaving me, the Branches, and Mr. Bolt.

Corbin motioned for me to take the chair.

"Oh no. We roshambo for it," I said.

"We what?"

I fisted my right hand and placed it on top of my flat left one. "In English, rock, paper, scissors…roshambo. It saves lives and settles arguments. MamaBear and I do this for dishes or settling who takes out the trash. First throw wins."

He threw scissors and I clapped paper. "Best two out of three," he suggested. He put his hands out again.

"Not a chance, bub." I dropped into the beanbag.

Corbin sat in the armchair as the couch filled up. He reached over and hauled the beanbag closer. My heart pittered and my brain pattered.

"Hey, Corbin?" Shelby sat forward on the couch, leaning toward him. "You drive that old Mustang, right?"

He shifted in the chair, barely, toward me. "Yeah."

"My dad named me after his old Shelby Mustang."

"What year?" He scooched up.

My jaw tightened. Don't overreact. He's a friendly guy.

"Uh, 1970, I think." Shelby spun a piece of her hair around her finger. I had to admit, her flowy, lace top was far cuter than my plain black T-shirt. Same with her stack-heeled boots.

"Same year as mine."

Her hand flew to his knee. "No way!"

I glanced to Corbin, who smiled at Shelby. No, down here on the beanbag, dummy.

"My dad would love to see your car. His got wrecked before I was born," she said.

"Anytime," he drawled.

I pushed my hands under my butt and stared at the tear starting in my jeans. Pinching the tiny Styrofoam balls flat with my fingers through the beanbag material, my toes bounced. In the dark corners of my mind, I already knew I didn't stand a chance.

His big Converse banged against my boots, interrupting my rambling, doomed thoughts. I stopped and looked up.

"You okay?" The hand closest to me dropped from the armchair and brushed my elbow. His dimple chased my doubts away as soon as it appeared.

"Yup."

Drama. I was worse than Madison.

Twenty

WHEN FRIDAY ROLLED AROUND, IT FELT LIKE THE DAY of "give-tests-in-every-subject-since-it's-the-last-day-before-vacation." How did I get the teachers who never showed movies? Corbin laughed at my fate since he only had two papers assigned. He ushered me to the Mustang, hand on the small of my back, to spend time with Marigold before my shift.

Sheila waved me over as soon as we hit the lobby. "Tori! Look!" She pulled me by the arm to the wall opposite of Jamie. The article featuring me and Marigold was printed and now proudly displayed in a thick black frame on the blue wallpaper.

"That's fancy." I truly didn't appreciate my face being blown up to almost life-size. But Marigold's smile made it better.

"I've also made a couple of calls to the local radio and television stations." She adjusted the lobby chair a bit. "I'm hoping to hear back from them soon."

My stomach bottomed out. "Can't they interview Marigold and not me?" Kids from school would see it. Ugh.

Corbin touched my elbow. "Come on, Tor. It'll be fine."

"You'll be wonderful! Besides, it's high time other kids saw what a good example you are by getting your school credits here. Speaking of…" Sheila hustled to Jamie's desk and rifled through a stack of papers. "Here. I almost forgot to give this to you for November's hours for school credit."

Honestly, I had no idea anyone was keeping track. "Uh, thanks."
I folded it nicely and put it into my jacket pocket.

"I'll call your mom and let her know if the news reporters want
to interview you."

I stuffed my response down. Let Sheila be happy. It's not like
joy ran down the halls at Willow Springs, unless you counted the
one time a naked guy got loose after his shower.

Corbin's hand brushed against mine as we walk to Marigold's
room. I tried not to think about it, how it'd feel to lace our fingers
together. Instead, I made sure to say hello to Harold and Jasmine.

"Mr. Dallas and Victoria Grace. Come in, come in." Marigold's
eyes were brilliant and her hair combed flat. "You are particularly
early today."

"Minimum day at school." I carefully lowered myself to my
chair. "And yahoo here hasn't packed for his trip to Texas and they
leave in a few hours." I jerked my thumb to the boy across the table
from me.

He smiled. "I like to live dangerously."

My phone vibrated.

MamaBear: Got a sec?

Yup. Chillin with Corbin and Marigold before work.

**MamaBear: Checked out the finances and your bank
account. Put in your two week notice with your boss. You can
get another job after Christmas.**

What? This had to be wrong. I slid my phone to Corbin. "Read
this."

His lips moved as he read it. "Cool."

"What's cool?" Marigold strained to see over his shoulder from
her bed.

"Her mom told her to quit the job at the theater," he said,
returning the phone to me.

Marigold clapped once. "Good. That boss is a flat tire."

I had no idea what that meant, but I laughed. Then I read the
text again. Crazy.

Are you joking?

MamaBear: Nope.

You're scaring me.

MamaBear: That didn't take much.

MamaBear: And we can start car shopping. Should find a good buy since it's close to Christmas.

Part of my brain exploded. I didn't even say anything before I shoved my phone back to Corbin.

"Dang. It's like an early Christmas for you." He wiggled the phone in the air toward Marigold. "She gets to start looking for a car, too."

"Do you already have your license to drive, Victoria Grace?"

"Yeah. Got it in March." I stared at MamaBear's words. Any minute now, she'd type, "Just kidding, sucker." It was too good to be true.

MamaBear: You pass out?

No. Trying to figure out if this is a big, fat joke.

MamaBear: It's not. I promise. I want you to spend more time with Marigold.

It all clicked with the words MamaBear didn't type: before she dies.

"I need a piece of paper to write my resignation," I said.

"I'll go get one from the car." Corbin was out of the door before I could protest.

Marigold gazed from the empty doorframe to me with a smile. "He's dead gone on you, child."

My face warmed. "I think so."

"Oh-ho. What happened?" She grinned and leaned forward.

"Nothing." I twisted the phone in my hands. "Well, he said he liked me."

"That's not nothing." Marigold snuck a peek to the hallway. "How did he say it?"

I suddenly felt like I was gossiping with my best friend. "Exactly what I said—called me weird and said that he liked me."

"Not exactly the most romantic boy, but good for him." Her eyes glittered with excitement. "What'd you say?"

"Uh…" I tried to remember while the feeling of molten lava spread through my body, when I thought of that night. "I told him that he said it perfectly."

"Excellent." Her scrutiny darted to the door when Corbin's voice floated down the hallway as he greeted residents and nurses. "Quiet now, I wouldn't want to embarrass the boy."

He walked in with a notebook. "I almost forgot these." He pulled out one colorful origami crane after another, lining them in a neat row on Marigold's nightstand. "Eight to represent your family." They were arranged tallest to shortest.

Marigold's eyes flooded. She gingerly took the one closest to her, the smallest. "For little Thomas, then." She pressed her lips against the green paper. "Thank you, Corbin."

"My pleasure, Miss Marigold."

After he handed me the notebook and a pen, I wrote my letter in perfect penmanship:

> *Mr. Bolt,*
>
> *Please accept my letter of resignation, effective two weeks from today. Thank you for having me on staff at the theater.*

When we got up to leave, Marigold arranged her crane family into different spots.

"What made you think of making those for her?" I asked.

Corbin opened the lobby door. "I was practicing. After the fourth or fifth one, I thought it'd be fun to make them smaller and smaller. Then, it looked like a family." He pulled open the Mustang door for me. "Funny thing is, I didn't even plan on eight. I happened to make them and thought of Marigold."

"You're a nice guy."

"Don't spread rumors." I wasn't sure I'd ever get tired of that dimple. Or those eyes.

It was a short drive to the theater. I wanted to hurry in and give my notice, but it'd be the last time I'd see Corbin for over a week.

"So," I said as he pulled into a parking stall, "try not to get bit by a rattlesnake."

"Don't plan on it. Plus, I have a fifty percent less chance." He knocked a knuckle against his plastic calf above his metal ankle.

"Nice. Have a safe drive down and send lots of pics. Especially of Sheba and the house, once you have the lights up." I sat still, waiting for him to possibly lean over.

"Will do. Have fun tonight." His right hand landed across the back of my seat, fingers brushing the collar of my jacket. I wanted to rest my head against his wrist, but remembered his scars. Probably would be pushing it.

Maybe after Thanksgiving I'd work up the courage to kiss him, because I might graduate at the rate he was going. "Of course. Gotta go quit my job."

There was a spring in my step when I walked into work. Mr. Bolt bustled around the lobby with a small vacuum and stopped long enough for me to hand him the note and walk away. There's no way I'd clock in late for the next two weeks.

———— ◦ ————

Six hours later, reeking of oil from a popcorn machine malfunction and tired from running one person short on the cleaning crew, I stood outside. My breath curled in white puffs while I scrolled through car ads online, waiting for MamaBear.

She came blasting into the parking lot. People stared, but I could tell she was in a hurry. We took off as soon as my door closed. "We're busy tonight. I gotta kick you to the curb at home and take off."

"No problem," I said.

"You smell like a dumpster."

My pants and shirt were stained. "Already know that."

She drove like a race car driver. I'd be grounded if I drove like that. "So…you and Corbin," she said on a sharp left turn.

My head banged against the window. "Ouch. Yes."

"Anything I should be worried about?"

"No." It was dark and she couldn't see my ears turning pink.

"I don't need to sit him down and threaten his life?"

"Mom! No. It's not like that."

MamaBear snorted. "It never is. But he seems like a good kid." She stopped on the road in front of the apartments. "Out you go. Everyone is kung-fu fighting tonight and I've gotta get to a DV."

I hopped out. "Love you. Have a safe shift."

"See you in the morning."

As she sped away, I sent a text to Corbin.

You get your laundry done in time?

Corbin: I can always buy socks in Texas.

I unlocked the door and was happy the heater had kicked on earlier. Double-checking the bolts, I shed my clothes and put them straight into the laundry basket. MamaBear would kick my butt if I used the washing machine two doors down late at night. I grabbed a couple of towels from the linen closet. The big hole on the top shelf, where my comforter used to be, made me happy.

Corbin: How'd Mr. Bolt take the news?

He ignored me. Best.Shift.Ever.

Trio wrapped herself around my bare leg. "Oh no, you don't get to pee on my towel this time, cat." I nudged her out of the bathroom with my foot and shut the door. The hot water relaxed my muscles, and the minty shampoo rid me of all butter-flavored smell. Wrapped in towels, I found a clean pair of pajama bottoms and MamaBear's old Newsboys T-shirt, circa 1994.

Corbin: Watching a movie. Grammy is already asleep.

The picture he sent showed her in an eye mask, her mouth wide open.

Does she snore?

Corbin: Like a freight train. I have earplugs. Or I leave my earbuds in with my sound app.

My earbuds hurt my tiny ears.

I added a sad face emoji and slapped a PB and J together. It wasn't quite like Grammy's tacos, but it would do. At least there was root beer. I poured myself a tall glass, slurping the foam when it spilled over.

Corbin: I got a new pair last year that have fitted earpieces. Is that one word or two? Earpieces. Ear pieces.

My eyes watered when the soda bubbled into my nose. The towel wrapped around my hair came flying off when I shook my head to get rid of the burning sensation in my nostrils.

One word. They sound fancy.

Our meaningless chat lasted long after I'd crawled under my covers and plugged in my phone. The texts got further and further apart as I drifted off to sleep until my phone buzzed in my hand.

Corbin: Gotta go. Supposed to be up in two hours for the flight.

STBY

My throat hurt. And the tripod cat pawed at my face. "Get off me, stupid cat." She kneaded into my chest, poking me with her claws. "I hate you," I mumbled, though I didn't, thrashing my arms and legs under the blankets to get her to go away.

As much as I wanted to, I couldn't fall back asleep. My mouth felt like moldy cheese probably tasted, but my bed was comfortable and I wasn't about to actually get up. I found my phone under the pillow and pulled it out.

Corbin sent me a picture of the sunrise through the plane window. I'd never been on a plane. I zoomed in and saw ice on the edges of the oval panel. The sun, stretching yellow and orange, fought its way through an opening in long, dark clouds.

Corbin: Good morning.

The next picture looked like the plane was landing on top of a freeway lit with headlights.

Corbin: In Phoenix, the planes drive over the cars on their own roads.

His legs extended to another chair inside a terminal in the next snap. Beyond the giant feet, people stared at their phones and tablets, and planes hooked up to the tunnel thingies.

Corbin: Layovers are my favorite.

Hey. How long are you stuck there?

Corbin: Well good morning. Finally. Must be nice to sleep in.

Don't be bitter because you're stuck in an airport.

Corbin: Actually we are boarding. I must turn off all electrical devices.

A blurry pic of the inside of the plane popped up.

Corbin: Landing after 1:30. Talk to you then.

Take a nap!

When my stomach finally made me emerge from my blanket cocoon, I saw MamaBear's bedroom door was closed. My painful earbuds went in so that I could watch the newest episode of a police cold case show. A commercial popped up for a free two-week trial of an ancestry site. I glanced down the hallway and wanted to ask MamaBear if she'd sign me up while I was on vacation. Maybe I could get more information on Daisy or the other kids. But she was still asleep, so I rinsed my cereal bowl in the sink.

My shift started at three. I slid my laptop into my backpack and got dressed for work. Through the curtains, dark clouds covered the sky, but rain wasn't in the forecast. I shimmied into a sweatshirt, inhaled a protein bar, and left a note for MamaBear on the counter with my request. It'd be so cool to find Marigold's family before Christmas. I biked to Marigold's to see if she was up for a walk in the hallway.

Jasmine was in her room and saved me a minute of waiting. Marigold was asleep, oxygen puffing through her canula. I had set up the laptop on the table when MamaBear sent me the log on and password for the ancestry site.

You know I love ya!

MamaBear: Yeah, yeah. Find her sisters and brother.

I quietly worked, creating a new profile with Marigold's info. I snuck out and found Sheila. She helped and gave me Marigold's date of birth. Little leaves popped up, telling me that I had hints, people who might be related. My fingers flew through the suggestions, discounting most of them but finding a few exciting clues. There was Daisy, but also a tidbit on their dad.

I found the family tree from the school library. Now that I had a log on, I could contact the person who posted the information. I typed an email, then erased it. After the third try, I was happy with the wording and sent it. Maybe she was logged on right now and would reply.

"Well, good afternoon." Marigold's voice was weighted with sleep. "How long have you been here?"

I slowly closed the laptop. "Not long." No need to make her suspicious.

My phone dinged. The beautiful house I'd seen in Corbin's phone filled my telephone screen.

Corbin: Home.

A few seconds later, another picture came. His fingers were spread across the black dog's head. The dog almost seemed like she was smiling.

Corbin: My Sheba girl.

I moved to Marigold's bed and showed her the pictures as they came in: the colossal porch, massive oak trees that made Sheba resemble an ant, the wood-planked living room and grand staircase to the second floor. Last, he sent a picture of a picture.

Corbin: Show this to M. This is my great-grandma and grandpappy at their first Thanksgiving together.

It was a black-and-white photo of a couple sitting for dinner. The woman wore a fancy hairdo, rolled high on her head, while the man carved a turkey in his military uniform.

I smiled. I knew exactly what I'd be wearing for our Thanksgiving dinner in room 1206.

Twenty-One

IT WAS HARD TO KEEP MY EXCITEMENT AT BAY. I WANTed to search for dress and hair ideas, or at least send MamaBear a text with my idea. Instead, I moseyed next to Marigold down the hall to show her the article posted in the lobby. She clung to my arm on the trip back, fingers digging into my muscles. I helped her back into bed.

"Thank you," she wheezed, as I moved her canula into place. "Thus goes my plans for the Turkey Trot this year."

"The marathon?" Redding always held the race on Thanksgiving morning, rain or shine. Never wanted to exert that much energy when I could be sleeping in.

Marigold nodded, coughing into her fist.

"I'll take you." The words rushed out of my mouth without waiting for my brain to catch up. "We'll use a wheelchair, figure out how to put your oxygen tank on it, and I'll push you." I needed to ask Sheila how to get it arranged. "And that'll give you plenty of time for a nap before dinner. MamaBear already bought the turkey."

"I can order the meal from the grocery market." She fussed with the edge of the comforter after I pulled it to her waist.

"Too late. We have olives and a bag of potatoes. The yams are canned, and we don't use onions on our green beans."

"Sounds delicious. But you must let me help with the expenses."

"Nah, it's already done. Would you like to have dinner here or at our apartment?" I would even clean my room to show her.

She patted my hand. "I wouldn't want to be an inconvenience. Let's plan on a little meal here, in case…well, there are nurses here."

My stomach dove like the first drop on a roller coaster. "Okay. We'll bring plates and silverware, too. Make it all fancy." I could do this—I would make it her best Thanksgiving.

Her breath was ragged, and her cheek twitched like she was trying to hide pain. Marigold leaned back into the pillows and regarded the atrium. "Could you put on my headphones for me?"

I got her all set up and lowered the head of the bed a little. Her weary eyes slid shut, one knobby hand on the corner of my comforter and the other covering her little tablet.

When her breath evened out, I took a picture and sent it to Corbin.

Went for a stroll to the lobby and back.

I pulled up a few websites and flipped through pictures. The fancy hair-do I wanted was called a Victory Roll and required lots of hairspray and bobby pins. I had to talk MamaBear into playing along.

I have an idea for Thanksgiving.

Three different pictures of ladies in dresses and hats from the '40s were sent to her, one after the other. Then the hair styles. I checked the clock on the laptop. I didn't have enough time or money to order and ship any dresses, but maybe the thrift store downtown could help me out with what I needed.

I switched tabs on my laptop and filled out the registration online for the Turkey Trot, the walking portion. No need to overdo it. Besides, Marigold would probably like to take everything in.

Marigold still slept when I left. I found Sheila at her desk and filled her in on my plans for the Trot. She furiously jotted notes. "Don't worry! I'll have it all ready by the night before." I gave myself a mental high five.

It wasn't until a few hours into my shift, during my first break, that Corbin sent me a text. I ignored MamaBear's messages.

Corbin: Sorry. Was out in the fields with Elisio fixing fences.

Sounds thrilling.

Corbin: It was more like fix two fences and drive the Jeep around the pasture.

Slacker.

Corbin: True. I had a nap too. Supper time now.

Corbin: Tell M hi.

I switched to MamaBear's texts. If I could come up with the outfits, she said she'd wear one too.

Oh, and I signed up for the Turkey Trot. Going to push Marigold in the walk portion. Want to come?

MamaBear: Good. I'd fear for her life if you pushed her while you ran. You and your random gravity checks. And sure.

She had to bring that up. It wasn't always my fault I ended up on the floor during basketball games.

Mr. Bolt ignored me for the second day. Fine by me. A Pixar movie opened, and my night felt like every kid had thrown their popcorn. On purpose. Don't even get me started on the bathrooms. Did all kids use that much toilet paper?

Before midnight, I biked home and let myself into the apartment. I wanted food, shower, and bed, in that order. By the time I cradled my phone in my hands, after the covers were pulled up to my chin, I could barely read my texts. Corbin's had come while I was in the shower.

Corbin: You're probably asleep, but goodnight.

Almost.

Corbin: Grew up here. Love it here. But can't wait to get back.

I smiled into my pillow.

Buenos noches, señor.

———┤ • ├———

I was a Slacker McSlack Pants and skipped church. The thrift store didn't open until ten AM, and I went back to bed after breakfast. And I probably would've slept longer, except someone rubbed my shoulders until I woke from a dream. Trio meowed from somewhere.

MamaBear perched on the edge of my bed. "It's ten."

"I was riding an elephant with a red saddle. And there was a monkey."

"You're so weird. Come on, get up." MamaBear plodded to the kitchen and soon, I could smell coffee.

After a stretch and a yawn, I pulled on a pair of jeans. "You wanna come with me to look for dresses?"

"You'll have to ride over. I gotta head to work a little early."

"If I had a car, I could drive over." I joined her at the coffeemaker.

"And if your dad wasn't a chump, we wouldn't have this conversation." MamaBear sipped her coffee as loudly as possible. "Don't be a chump. Be patient. We'll go on Tuesday."

I showed her the pictures Corbin sent the day before, along with the sunrise from the ranch. She didn't say anything, but her silence meant that she wanted to ask questions.

"He hasn't even tried to hold my hand." There. Now she knew everything.

"I didn't say anything," she said.

"No, but you wanted to."

She grinned into her mug. "I gotta go get dressed for work."

After biking to the store, I hunted the dress rack and picked a few options. I tried on a navy dress with teeny tiny polka dots. I talked with the cashier about my idea. She disappeared into the back and rolled out a rack of clothes.

"These haven't been sorted, so the sizes are all jumbled up, honey." The clerk waved at the stand.

Thirty minutes later, I'd not only found perfect dresses, but a cream-colored hat with a netted veil for MamaBear. The cashier remembered something in the back room and returned with a small tan hat with white ribbon roses, called a fascinator. I added it to my bag. "It'll be perfect for Marigold."

—————⊣ • ⊢—————

The rest of the week passed in video calls to Corbin, visits to Marigold, rearranging the Thanksgiving supplies on the counter, texts to Corbin, buying safety pins to alter the dresses, and getting my Victory Rolls perfected.

Thanksgiving morning, I was up by six. Forty percent chance of rain. I tucked my umbrella into my backpack. I tugged on my warm-up pants, a blue flannel over a thermal shirt, and Corbin's beanie.

MamaBear met me at the coffeemaker and slid a cup to me. "Two miles, huh?"

"You think you're up for it?"

"Watch your mouth, kid."

I loved it when she quoted movies to me. "No problem, Han Solo."

It took us longer to load and unload Marigold, probably because we kept asking if she was okay every thirty seconds. "You're worse than Sheila," she mumbled after I fidgeted with her footrest for the second time.

At check-in, I took the number and pinned it to Marigold's jacket. MamaBear and I had to roshambo to see who would push her. I won. The lady checking us in offered to take a picture, which I sent to Corbin. We joined the sea of families at the start line.

"So many people," Marigold said, adjusting her canula.

MamaBear tucked in the edges of the blanket she'd draped around Marigold's shoulders. She straightened and scanned the crowd. "Yup." She always examined places. It was just my

MamaBear being all MamaBear, protecting me like she had her entire life.

The start was a surge of bodies forward, a jumble of strollers and families dressed in matching shirts. We leisurely walked the trail. Marigold remained quiet but inspected everything: the river, the wild bushes, and the people who passed us by. I double-checked the oxygen to make sure the flow was correct. If I asked her again if she was okay, she would've swatted at me.

After the mile marker, she sighed, the breath disappearing in the morning fog. "I forget how much life there is, being cooped up in my room."

I followed her observant gaze. A pair of yellow-and-brown birds darted from tree to tree, arguing to each other in bird talk. The river gurgled and sped by. Behind and in front of us, laughter echoed down the river trail.

Marigold may have forgotten, but I was too embarrassed to admit that I'd never paid attention.

A couple of hours later, Marigold was back in her room and we returned to the apartment. MamaBear won the first shower when she showed scissors to my paper. I used the time to fuss over my outfit.

As I turned off the shower, I heard my phone chirping. I didn't expect a video call, but wrapped a towel and ran to my bedroom, my hair dripping down my face. And I certainly didn't expect the caller.

"Nicky!"

"Hey, Squirt." My cousin's face was pixelated, but I could barely make out his smile. "You ladies getting ready to sit down for dinner?"

"MamaBear is checking the turkey now." I held the phone out in front of me and ran to the kitchen for her to see. "Look who it is, Mom!"

She twisted her face up from the open oven door. "Nick. Oh

my word, Bubby." Her voice melted, and tears gathered in her eyes. "I'm so happy to see your face."

"Don't cry, Aunt Kasey. Everything here is okay." The delay made his lips move after the words came out of the speaker. "I don't have long. I traded in a favor to make a quick call."

We both crowded the screen. "We love you and wish you were here," MamaBear said.

"We are going to have dinner with Marigold." I'd told him about her in emails.

"Have fun and eat some for me. I gotta go. I love you both and I'll try to call again."

We both waved like performing monkeys at the phone screen until it blipped to black.

MamaBear wiped the corners of her eyes. "That made my day. Let's get my hair done."

Her hair took me a couple of times to get right, but it finally fell into three perfect rolls. I pinned the tiny hat in place, grateful I'd bought two packages of bobby pins. She didn't want to change into her button-up dress until after dinner was in the containers and ready to go.

I finished my hair in one try. The navy dress I'd picked had the zipper in the back, but I was able to get it by myself. If anyone examined it closely, they'd see the safety pins along the seams, but it fit well and the full skirt billowed up when I twirled in front of the mirror. The collar felt weird because it brushed against the sensitive skin above my collarbone. I slipped on MamaBear's black flats and worked on my makeup. A little cat-eye eyeliner, curled eyelashes with mascara, a swipe of cherry red lipstick, and I was ready.

I stepped out to show MamaBear. "Dang, you clean up nice!" She was a mash-up of Victory Rolls, a plaid flannel shirt with paint splatters, and spandex shorts as she load containers of food into paper bags. "Lemme change and we can go."

She reappeared minutes later in a buttery-yellow dress with

tiny daisies. The tan pumps she used for court appearances really completed the outfit. "Lipstick?"

I carefully swiped the same red across her lips.

"I'm glad you met Marigold," she said once I stepped back to check the application. She didn't say anything more, but her silence wrapped my heart into a warm embrace. I couldn't imagine my life without Marigold.

We got the food, plates, and silverware to the car in a single trip. I snapped an exaggerated winking selfie for Corbin as we drove to Marigold's.

He replied with a heart emoji. And my own heart ran happy circles.

The nurses and aides at Willow Springs took pictures with their phones when we strolled down the hall.

Marigold was waiting, upright in bed and hair smoothed down. Her mouth dropped open when she saw us. "Did I miss the dress code memo? You both look like firstclass dames."

"We brought you something, too." I carefully pinned the fascinator onto her hair. "Let me show you." I snapped a pic and turned the screen around.

"I'm all spiffy!" she exclaimed, reaching up to touch her hat.

One of the employees who crowded the doorway took several pictures of the three of us, MamaBear crouching on one side of the bed and me on the other. I sent one to Corbin.

"We usually didn't wear hats in the Canteen when we served meals." Marigold reached up to touch the roses. "But there always is an exception to the rule. And it is certainly less crowded with only a few of us in my room."

"Were you usually at the Canteen for Thanksgiving?" I carefully unwrapped the plates and put them on the counter.

"Not usually. It was only open for three years. It was such a little sacrifice of time to give back to the men serving our country. Besides, we weren't always there."

"Was your mistress busy with films?" MamaBear took the lid off of the turkey, and it smelled like I should hurry up and eat.

"Only one. Mostly, the USO tour took up her time overseas."

"Oh no." I rummaged back through all of the bags. "I forgot glasses for the sparkling cider."

"There are glasses above the sink, Victoria Grace. Let's use the fancy pink ones."

I pulled down the frosted pink goblets. They had to be from the '80s, but they would do.

The turkey was moist and the yams nice and mushy. Marigold ate tiny portions of everything and finished it all, declaring the green beans her favorite.

"Yes, I worked hard on those," MamaBear said. "I opened the can, poured the beans into a bowl, and used the microwave."

After the plates were cleared, I poured the last of the cider equally among the three of us. Marigold studied her glass. I was about to ask if she needed anything when she spoke.

"When I was a girl, we had a tradition. We'd go around the table and say one thing we are thankful for. It can be whatever you want." Her eyes landed on me. "You first."

I wouldn't cry. Marigold needed me to smile. "I'm thankful for being able to be here with you and MamaBear today." My hand shook and little bubbles of cider burst on the surface. I'd made it without bursting into tears.

MamaBear tilted her cup of cider in the air. "I'm thankful for family. And I'm praying that Nicky is safe right now."

When Marigold cleared her throat, I could barely swallow. I bit my bottom lip to keep it from quivering. "I am thankful I can spend my last days with such wonderful friends. I finally have family again."

I knew the tears would ruin my perfect eyeliner.

And that was okay with me.

Twenty-Two

SUNDAY'S SERMON AFTER THANKSGIVING WENT IN one ear and out the other. MamaBear was working, and I'd biked to church. I kept checking the time. Then, I'd check the flight status. After that, I'd recheck to make sure I didn't miss any texts. I avoided Pastor Matt after he locked eyes with me after the service by ducking into the restroom. Safely locked in the stall, I checked it all again.

Corbin: Storms have everything delayed. Our flight might get bumped.

I filled a line with crying and sad emojis. Nothing else I could do.

The damp air didn't bug me as I pedaled home. I changed directions a block from home and turned toward Willow Springs. Being with Marigold would be better than sitting home, obsessing about how I could be a better air traffic controller than the guys in Texas. They were probably shining their belt buckles instead of figuring out how to get people home. And I needed me a certain dimple.

Monday morning, I was exhausted. Every hour, I'd checked my phone for a text. At least I was in my bed. Corbin was probably slumped over in a chair or curled up on nasty airport floor.

Swallowing my pride, I took the bus to school, knowing I could get a ride home in his Mustang. Looking forward to the squeaking wipers and worn carpet was the only thing that kept me sane on the ride. My phone pinged as the bus ejected its students at the curb.

Corbin: We're in Sacramento. They boarded us fast. I didn't have time to text.

I wanted the kids in front of me to move quicker. The day needed to hurry up.

Corbin: I'll see you at lunch.

Good. Because I rode the bus to school.

Corbin: STBY

Every class lasted ten hours in my mind. I'm sure the second hand went backwards a few times. I barely remembered to write down the homework assignments.

And then the lunch bell rang.

Fuzzy, warm feelings buzzed my entire brain and body when I walked out of Creative Writing and saw him waiting for me. I knocked my shoulder into his bicep. "Hey."

"Hey." Dimpled goodness greeted me.

Our conversation was cut short when Madison found us on the way to the lockers and blurted, in obsessive detail, about her trip to the Bay Area. We settled for sitting side by side at the table, elbows touching, making sure to comment when Mads stopped for breath.

"Corbin. You skipped Geometry?" Shelby stopped on the way to her table.

"Flights were delayed. Got back a half hour ago."

She leaned over the table. I cringed and stared at my sandwich. Come on. Put your assets back into your plunging neckline. "How was Texas?" Wait a second. How'd she know he was in Texas?

"Decent. How was your Thanksgiving?"

"Good. I'll text you the homework from Geometry." Shelby smiled her perfect smile and trotted off to her groupies.

I needed to know. "Didn't know you guys had a class together."

"She flunked last year. She's failed a few tests, even when she cheats and gets the answers from my paper." He nabbed a pretzel from my lunch. "I don't know how she's passing this year."

I glanced up at Shelby's ultra-skinny jeans. "Oh, I have an idea," I muttered into my sandwich.

———┤ • ├———

Monday ended, and that meant Car Shopping Tuesday! MamaBear and I spent the afternoon on the laptop, sending texts and emails to possibilities. She tried to get the price lower on the first two we found later in the evening, but we went home empty-handed. And I was a grouch who still owned nothing more than a bicycle.

The highlight of Wednesday, other than knowing it was only twenty-two days until Christmas, was youth group. No one returned any car emails or texts about cars. The person in charge of Daisy's family tree still hadn't replied. And my lunch was a protein bar because we'd eaten the last of the turkey the night before.

Pastor Matt loaded us all into the church van for a coffee shop run. Corbin held the door open while everyone dodged the rain and jumped in. I was about to nab the front bench seat to sit next to him when Shelby ducked under my arm.

"'Scuse me."

Sitting next to her while she twisted around in the seat to talk with Zane and Hunter wasn't exactly the idea I had in mind, but it was a short ride. I hopped out as soon as Pastor Matt put the van into park. It was almost as bad as the school bus.

Corbin grabbed a couple of chairs in the corner. We compared car ads on our phones until Shelby took the last chair next to us. What was with her? She was suddenly like a sock with static cling, showing up wherever she wasn't needed.

She pulled out her own phone. "Whatcha guys doin'?" Her case was a bedazzled nightmare.

I reminded myself to play nice with others. "Looking at cars."

"I remember my first car. Poor thing didn't stand a chance against the truck." She peeped over her phone at Corbin. "Texting and driving is illegal for a reason."

"Glad no one was hurt." He swallowed hard, his jaw muscles flexing. Duh. She had no idea about his family.

"Just my car, rest in pieces."

Amelia, for lack of any chair to sit in, dropped into Shelby's lap. "Hey, bae." Shelby and Amelia lapsed into a rehash of a trashy show they binged watched over the weekend.

And although it wasn't a particularly Christian thing to say, I mumbled, "Good riddance." From the corner of my eye, Corbin's grin made me feel better.

On Thursday, I was grumpy after two days of useless car hunting. Corbin promised to take me to Marigold's after school to see if she'd let us decorate for Christmas. Seemed he had the bug to string up lights after Texas.

When the lunch bell rang, he wasn't at the lockers, but that wasn't unusual. Sometimes he'd wait at the table with Madison. I swapped my books for my lunch and hurried to the cafeteria.

My eyes went straight to the curls sticking out from under his beanie. But my feet stopped outside of the door. My throat was suddenly dry and my stomach rolled. I was going to barf.

Corbin sat with his back against the table, long legs in the aisle. Perched like a beautiful, dark songbird on his thighs, Shelby laughed and tossed her hand onto his shoulder.

And he smiled his dimpled smile at her.

No.

She tilted toward his chest and hung her hand around his neck. Their noses nearly touched. Shelby nabbed his beanie and thrust it on her head.

Stop.

Corbin placed one hand flat on the bench. The other curled around Shelby's pink sweater at her waist.

My chest squeezed. My feet stepped backwards until my

shoulders collided with the wall. Though my brain begged to turn away, my eyes locked onto the pair.

Shelby grabbed both sides of his face. She lowered her lips to his.

I spun toward my locker and pulled out my books and phone.

Mom I have to leave school.

MamaBear: You sick?

I'll explain. I'm going to throw up.

I pushed out of the doors and practically ran to the parking lot.

MamaBear: Tori. What's wrong?

I am walking home. Please call the office.

MamaBear: Tell me now.

The first sob bubbled out at the edge of the asphalt. I slapped a hand over my mouth.

He didn't like me after all.

———⌐•⌐———

The apartment door opened as soon as I stepped onto the sidewalk. I fell onto her shoulder, blubbering. It hurt, more than anything I'd ever known. My head throbbed. My body ached. And nothing mattered besides the pain of being tossed aside.

"Tell me what happened." MamaBear led me by the shoulders to the bathroom. She dunked a washcloth under cold water and wrung it before mopping my face.

My head shook back and forth. I couldn't. She thought he was a good guy.

"It's not an option. You need to tell me."

My words spewed in spurts and sobs. I slid down the wall in the hallway and sat, using the washcloth as a tissue.

"Maybe it's a misunderstanding."

What a joke. I told her and she took his side. I didn't even try to stop my sound of disgust.

"I'm just saying. He doesn't seem like the kind of guy who would do that," she said.

"I can't believe…never mind."

"I believe you, Tori. It's hard because…" MamaBear's voice hitched and ground to a stop. "I hate to see you with a broken heart."

She needed to shut up. I wanted to crawl into her lap and fold my legs up, feeling her strong arms flex around me. I wanted my stupid, stupid chest to quit aching—to quit longing. It wasn't my broken heart. It couldn't be my heart because I hadn't said the "L-O-V-E" word yet, and neither had he.

My head thrummed in pain, right behind my eyeballs. The carpet in the hall wasn't comfortable, but I didn't want to move. If I stayed still, maybe everything would fix itself.

I knew MamaBear was still there without opening my eyes, leaning against the wall. She probably looked sad, her eyebrows barely pulled together. When I finally cracked my eyes, her hands were in her jean pockets, and she inhaled deeply.

"I'm only your mom, so I know how shallow this sounds, but I'm sorry, Tor." She crouched and touched my knees. With a quick squeeze, she stood up and went into her bedroom, the door left open.

My nose wouldn't stop running. I retreated to the bathroom and yanked a couple of tissues from the box.

MamaBear zipped up her equipment bag in her bedroom while I blew my nose. She appeared in the doorway of the bathroom, hair pulled into a bun above her neck, wearing a tight black undershirt that always went under her bulletproof vest. "Stay busy."

Ah, great. She wanted me to do chores instead of mope. I should've known better. I scoffed and chucked the used tissue to the trash. I needed to fix my mascara.

"If there was anything I learned after…after your dad left, it was to stay busy." She caught my bloodshot eyes in the reflection of the mirror. "When you stop and think about it, it'll tear you up and drag you under."

Her words clicked like two abstract puzzle pieces meant only for the other.

"What do I do?" I whispered.

"Things you'd never dream of: wash the walls, scrub kitchen shelves. Dust and clean the ceiling fan. Scrub the corners in the kitchen floor. Be obsessive." MamaBear swallowed hard in the mirror. She was telling me what she had done. "It doesn't make it go away, but it helps. That, and loud music."

I smiled at her reflection before I took two steps and crumpled onto her shoulder. "Will you pay me?" I half-laughed and blubbered, inhaling the baby powder smell she used to keep the sweat to a minimum under all the layers of her uniform.

"Dream on, kid." Her bag dropped to the floor. She pulled back and took my face into her strong hands—hands trained to hold a gun, and hands that comforted children who were taken from abuse so horrible, she would never repeat it. MamaBear was my gravity. "I will bring home mint ice cream, though."

"Have a safe shift. Love you." I leaned forward and did something I hadn't done in a long time—I kissed her on the cheek.

Tears crowded her eyes. "Love you too, Tori." She softly slapped my cheek and retrieved her bag before walking to the front door. "Don't forget to clean on top of the fridge," she called over her shoulder, pulling the door shut.

Trio wobbled out from the living room and let out the saddest meow ever when she left. And I felt that in my soul.

———— ◦ ————

The kitchen was my first target. I wiped and washed. It was easy to ignore the incoming text sounds with my music turned up to the point it nearly hurt my eardrums. But it did help me move from the kitchen to the living room in record time and chase away the fleeting thoughts of Corbin's lips pressed against Shelby's.

I'm not sure who I hated more.

After the living room was vacuumed, I pulled out my earbuds. Whoever designed those weapons of torture didn't have tiny ear canals. I'm sure I would've missed the knocking at the door if my ears hadn't stung.

Through the peephole, my worst confrontation literally arrived. Corbin's black beanie was back in place, pulled low. He raised his hand to knock again when I yanked the door open.

Everything I was going to say stuck in my throat. I wanted to scream at him, to rage at him for being the exact type of guy I hated. My mind tormented me with Shelby's laughter, his arm around her waist. And my tears didn't help.

"What?" It was the only word I could think of.

"Are you okay? You've been ignoring me—I've been sending texts since lunch."

How could he not figure it out? My chest burned and for half a second, I thought I might throw up or throw my first punch. "Are you kidding me?"

"Tori, I'm not standing here in the freezing rain for kicks and giggles."

My anger rolled and I blinked back my tears. I didn't have time for tears. I needed walls.

"Let me make it perfectly clear for you: Shelby."

Corbin's face scrunched together and his head shook back and forth a little. He was utterly confused. So typical of a guy.

My rage grew. "I was there in the cafeteria today and saw you and Shelby."

Like a cartoon lightbulb had gone off, he realized what I had seen. His face muscles went slack and he took a step forward. "She sat on my lap while I was waiting for you." From his tone of voice, either he was a good liar or was telling the truth.

"I'm not an idiot, Corbin."

"She skipped Geometry and asked me what the homework was. She flirts with anyone who will help her."

"I suppose the flirting and kissing was part of the Geometry homework." I waved air quotes in the air.

"She grabbed my face and I didn't even have time to stop her." His words came out faster. "Tori, please. You gotta believe me." He wrung his hands together. "I had my hand on her waist because the way she sat down shifted my prosthetic."

Part of my brain wanted to believe him. But I knew better. I would rather walk away than be rejected again. I didn't need to relearn living—I'd done it as a kid, wondering where Dad was and why he didn't come home.

A lump stalled my throat. My anger washed into embarrassment and bitterness. "I won't be hurt by you," I managed to whisper, before a sob surfaced.

Corbin's sigh came with a heavy mist. "I am so sorry."

A bitter laugh crept out. "Do you have any idea how stupid that sounds? That you're sorry?"

"How can I get you to understand that it didn't mean anything? I don't even like her as a person."

"But she kissed you!"

"I didn't kiss her back."

Stupid, stupid tears. I glanced to his work boots in the puddles. That way, he didn't have to see me cry. Because I knew he wasn't lying and I was being absurd.

"Tori." He hooked a finger under my chin and tilted it up. I sniffed before snot slid down my blotchy face. "I am going to kiss you now."

Maybe I should have closed my eyes, like in the movies, but I didn't—at first. I stared at his lips as they closed in—right up to the moment his thumb brushed my cheek. Then, my eyes closed as our lips touched.

There were no fireworks, no gobbling down each other's tongues, but my entire body felt like it had been pushed inches from a blazing campfire. I was toasty and breathless after Corbin kissed me gently and pulled back, his brown eyes bouncing back and forth between mine.

His hands wound around my back and pulled me into his flannel, damp and faintly smelling like Grammy's laundry detergent. My cheek pressed against his thudding heart. I felt him kiss the top of my head before resting his chin on my hair.

"I haven't said it yet because I've been waiting for the perfect moment and I screwed that up." Corbin lowered his lips. His breath tickled my ears. "I love you. You have permission to kick my butt if I'm ever that stupid again."

My laugh was muffled by his shirt. "Like I need your permission."

Twenty-Three

I REALLY TRIED TO BE SAD ON MY LAST DAY OF WORK.
Let me rephrase that: I tried to not be too happy when I clocked in for my last shift. Really, it was spectacularly hard to keep the grin off of my face when Mr. Bolt gave me a sweaty handshake and mumbled his best wishes to my future.

I pushed my broom through the theaters and vacuumed the lobby between the show sets. My last free bag of popcorn was slightly stale and oversalted. The only thing that even tweaked my heartstrings was saying goodbye to Aubrey, but I had her number.

Corbin pulled up thirty minutes before the end of my shift. Our first official date was planned: shopping for Christmas stuff for Marigold at the 24-hour store a few blocks from the movie theater. MamaBear approved. "It has surveillance cameras. I'm good."

He even let me open my own door and had the heaters on full blast when I sat down. "You ready?"

"Yeah." I'd changed into jeans and a sweater in the bathroom. My former work clothes, grungy from oil and washing, rested in the bottom of the trashcan. "I still smell like butter flavoring. I can't get the stench from my hair until I take a shower."

The vinyl seat squeaked as he leaned over. "I don't mind." He kissed me like a cowboy in a Hallmark movie, hands tangled in my hair, long enough to make my brain hiccup into a blank space. Not that I admitted to watching those kinds of movies.

It was a quick drive to the store. And while I should've been tired after my shift, my brain was running at top speed when we walked through the doors of the store and he reached over to hold my hand.

"Oh! This is my favorite Christmas song!" I grabbed a cart and pushed it like a skateboard as Nat King Cole crooned from the speakers high above. I started singing when the first verse started. "Chestnuts roasting on an open fire…"

We headed straight for the Christmas section, in all of its overstocked glory. One aisle held winter wonderland decorations while another displayed jewel-toned ornaments and feathers.

"Nothing screams 'Marigold' to me." Corbin plucked a pink, glitter-bombed pinecone from the shelf.

"Yeah, it'd be better if we could make ornaments like from the '40s or '50s, all vintage." A fragile-looking peacock with a real peacock feather tail caught my eye. "Like this."

We both pulled up different websites on our phones and searched for similar ornaments in the store. Other than the peacock, we found the stringy kind of tinsel and a small, pre-lit tree that would fit on Marigold's table. "I want to make sure she can see it from her bed." I didn't think she and I would be taking too many more walks.

"What about if we made the ornaments?" Corbin swiveled his phone to me. There were sequined balls and paper gingerbread cutouts on his screen.

"Oh, you want to show off your crafting skills." I pointed the cart toward the craft section.

"I am pretty crafty."

We picked several things that seemed like they would work. By "we," I mean that Corbin made the choices and I said, "That looks good."

Several bags later, because we had to go back and buy cute

lights for the windows and oil stuff for the diffuser, MamaBear sent a text to let me know it was time to head home.

Did you drive by to check if we were still here?

MamaBear: Absolutely.

---------‑•‑---------

The next morning, I sat next to Corbin and Grammy in church, instead of my normal spot. It was weird, because it felt like I was betraying the people who usually sat near me and said hello. But the worship leader's cool wife was in front of us. She had a nose ring too, and we compared studs.

My phone pinged at lunch with Corbin and Grammy at the diner.

Sheila: Sorry to bother u on Sunday but I got a msg from news chnl 8 and they want interviews today

My hash browns caught in my throat and I hacked until Corbin handed me a glass of water. I showed him the text while I dabbed my eyes.

"When?"

I shook my head, taking a few gulps.

What time?

Sheila: 2 can u make it?

My phone said 12:34. Technically, I could. But I didn't really want to and wished there was anything else important to do.

Yes.

Sheila: C u then

"What's going on? Another hot date at the thrift store this time?" Grammy shoveled a bit of pie in, grinning.

My face burned. "No," I sputtered. "Those letters that Marigold and I wrote? Sheila sent the article to the local news station and apparently they want to interview us at two today." It was embarrassing, but I had to swallow my pride and ask Corbin a totally "girl" question. "Can I get a ride home to change into clothing a bit more professional than a plain purple shirt and jeans?"

Corbin checked out my outfit. "You look fine."

Even Grammy rolled her eyes.

I grimaced. "Please?"

"Of course." He touched my fingers on the water glass. "You wanna come, Grammy?"

"That would be splendid. I could finally meet Miss Marigold."

Great. Let's all go.

They waited in the recently cleaned living room, while I pulled apart my closet because nothing was clean or fit or looked right. Finally, I kept my jeans on, mostly because they were my favorite dark pair, and settled on a fitted black sweater. My makeup was okay, but I added a tiny bit of blush to subdue the freckles.

"Would you like a bit of lipstick?" Grammy dug around in her gigantic purse that made my backpack resemble a coin pouch.

Did I need lipstick? I thought about it until MamaBear's bedroom door opened. "Tori?" She sounded like a frog when she woke up.

"Ah, sorry." Yeah. Forgot she was sleeping late. It was her eight-hour day. "We're leaving to go to Marigold's."

"Did you put perfume on?" She stayed in her doorway and called down the hall.

Thanks, Mom. "No, it's deodorant. We're going now."

"You might want to catch the five o'clock news." Grammy handed me a tube of lipstick, glancing down the hallway.

"Yeah?" MamaBear scratched her tangled bed head.

"The news crew is interviewing Tori and Marigold about their letters and the article."

Corbin watched like a guy at a tennis match, head bobbing between the voices. He gave me two thumbs and eyebrows up.

I opened the front door. "Okay, gotta go or we'll be late." If I didn't act quickly, MamaBear would be squeezed next to me in the backseat of the Mustang.

Corbin maneuvered into the parking space next to the news van. My stomach lurched. Was there some way I could get out of this? Even Corbin's hand against my back didn't calm my nerves.

Sheila buzzed around Willow Springs, from the lobby to the nurses' stations, picking up papers, helping residents back to their rooms. Poor cameraman. Didn't need to be blocked by Jasmine.

As it turned out, it wasn't a cameraman at all. It was a camera-woman. She was chatty, hurried, and her makeup looked like it was applied in layers.

I made quick introductions with Grammy and Marigold. Then I brushed Marigold's hair smooth. She didn't want her canula. Can't say that I blamed her. I knew the expression in those bright blue eyes. She didn't want to be remembered with plastic tubes in her nose.

The camerawoman pumped my hand up and down and barely touched Marigold's. She set up the camera at the foot of the bed. We hurried through questions she had written, basically rehashing exactly what the article in the lobby stated.

The reporter thrust the microphone at me. "How did you meet Marigold?"

I peeked at Corbin, then at Marigold. This might be the only time she'd hear me say it. I pushed my doubt down. I didn't care what the kids at school would say. "At first, I did it for the school credits." Marigold reached for my hand. "But then, I came because I wanted to. She told me stories about growing up in Hollywood and the war and traveling to Paris. I never had grandparents growing up." I paused. My throat felt crushed when I saw our hands.

"Okay, leave your hands like that." To the reporter, it was all business, a story. Our fingers, old and young, clipped nails and chipped black polish, woven together, was altogether different to me. "Why did you decide to write to the servicemen and women for the holidays?" She pulled out her phone and looked at a list of what I assumed were questions. It wasn't about Nicky or Marigold's soldiers for her. My heart for the gnarled hands in mine went beyond my answers to the bland, obvious inquiry.

Like a dust tornado, the newswoman wrapped up her interview, shook my hand, avoided Marigold's, and bade us farewell. "Make sure you watch it on the five-thirty news. I should have it edited and ready to go."

"Victoria Grace, my oxygen please." Marigold drooped into her pillows. I rushed to get the canula in place.

"Let's get her comfortable," Sheila said, moving to lower the headboard. "All worn out from your interview?"

Marigold's eyelids fluttered, her white eyelashes like tiny moths at a lightbulb. "Yes. But it was lovely. Simply lovely."

"I'll see you tomorrow, okay?" I tucked a stray hair behind the tubing at Marigold's ear.

Her eyes shifted back and forth between mine. She smiled and reached up to touch my face. "Such an unexpected blessing."

Grammy invited me to dinner, since MamaBear was working. Corbin and I printed out ornaments we wanted to make with Marigold. Grammy showed us a recipe to make cinnamon smelling dough that could be cut with cookie cutters and baked hard.

"Are you both in a conspiracy to convert me to crafting? I admit, I do have a little experience with pipe cleaner animals, but that's it."

Grammy served up leftovers, since she didn't cook on Sundays. We sat backwards at the kitchen bar, in order to see the television.

I almost dodged the bullet until the very last story came on. "And tonight, a special story about a friendship that has not only crossed generations, but overseas to our servicemen and women."

The reporter did a good job of editing. I sounded intelligent, which was good because I thought I had messed up the entire thing. The story ended with my voice talking over the shot of our clasped hands. "There's no one like Marigold." I didn't know the mic was live when I was talking with Grammy after their introductions, before the interview.

It was exactly how I felt. And I didn't know how I'd handle it once she was gone.

———┤ • ├———

It didn't bother me that Corbin didn't clobber me with PDA. I wasn't a particular fan of kids sucking each other's faces off in the hallway. I mean, the extent of our display of affection in public had been when I rode on the back bar of the shopping cart and he pushed my waist. Still, I hoped for a little change on Monday. I mean the "word" had been said. Maybe I'd get hand-holding privileges.

But Monday morning proved to be every bit the same as the week before. We joked on the ride to school, bumped into each other on purpose, and made goo-goo eyes before we left for class. Okay, so it was a tortoise race, but at least I knew the tortoise loved me.

I was itching for a fight by the time it was lunch knowing that Corbin got out of class with Shelby. I didn't want her near him. Ever. My back hurt from sitting straight up at the table, and I kept an eye on the doorways for her blonde hair.

"Do I need to remind you?" His voice at my ear startled me.

"What?"

"You look like you are ready to murder a certain person." He still leaned over.

I relaxed my shoulders. "I wouldn't do that here. Too many witnesses. And what do you want to remind me about?"

Corbin took my fist from the table and flattened it, palm up, onto the bench. He placed his fist over the top, and extended his thumb, index, and pinky finger, sign language for "I love you."

"I really don't want you to kick my butt," he whispered.

My raging estrogen levels came back into check for the rest of the day. In fact, I was freaking nice to people. Even the girl who crushed my foot because she was watching her phone instead of the hallway. "I'm okay," I called to her back. I was an angel.

We went to Marigold's after school, armed with our ornament printouts, lights for the windows and the tree.

"Victoria Grace and Mr. Dallas. You come in a pair now. That's nice." She winked at me as Corbin unloaded the supplies to the table. "What have you brought today?"

Corbin got to work assembling the little tree while Marigold and I studied the pictures. When he moved on to taping the lights in her window, she relaxed into the pillows.

"Are you okay? Need me to lower your bed?"

"No, dear. I have wanted to talk to you since you arrived and you seemed so happy about decorating that I didn't want to spoil it." She ran a finger across a photo of a newspaper star. "I had my follow-up appointment today with the specialist."

Inside, my head was shaking back and forth. The tone of her voice, her manners, everything was wrong.

"They've decided that I'm at class four."

The end stage. There was nothing they could do.

I could see my nostrils flare as I fought to keep calm. But I couldn't. I knelt next to her bed, held her hand, and cried. "I know I'm supposed to be strong, but give me a minute here."

"We still have a bit of time, dear." Her palm stroked the top of my head.

I sniffled. "Yeah. We have a tree to decorate. And you're going to teach me to make 'real' eggnog." From over my shoulder, Corbin handed me a tissue.

I knew the end would eventually come. It came for everyone, young or old. But I never wanted Marigold to leave. She'd planted herself into my heart, and it ached to think of coming around her doorway to an empty bed.

When my phone dinged, I was grateful to be able to turn to check it. An email. I swiped to open it.

Hello Tori. I apologize that it took me so long to respond. I've been out of the country traveling on business, and this email isn't checked often.

Your story is amazing. But I hope you understand my hesitation when I question the validity of your Marigold and the one from our family tree. It was our understanding that she moved to Europe or England to escape persecution.

Can you do me a favor? My cousin (Kate) and I want to make sure she is the right person. Can you ask her what her mother's name is? We have it written in a binder and decided never to publish it on the family tree.

I can't wait to hear from you.
        ~Patricia Jamison-Bettis

I clicked the reply box and typed my two-word response: Minoru Nippon.

I'd done it. I'd found Marigold's family.

Twenty-Four

CORBIN AGREED—WE NEEDED TO TELL MARIGOLD right away. However, knowing her heart was failing, we wanted to be careful. No need to give her a heart attack with the best news in the world.

"It's already the seventh of December. Wonder if they live nearby," Corbin whispered. He taped the last strand of lights to the window sill and plugged them in. When she woke, she'd be greeted with a colorful room. "Maybe they'd come before Christmas to meet her."

"December seventh." I sat forward, smiling. "We have to tell her today."

"Why?"

It was completely perfect. I clapped my hands to my mouth. "It's Pearl Harbor Day. Her birthday, but the day she pretty much lost her family." Mr. Hammond had reminded us in History about the significance of the day.

We used the cardboard backing from the lights to jot notes. I sent MamaBear a text letting her know and practically bounced in my chair until Marigold finally woke up.

She loved the lights. The colors glowed on her pale face. "How beautiful!"

I moved my chair next to her bed, laptop on my shoulder. I couldn't screw this up. "I have something I need to tell you."

Her gaze flitted from me to Corbin leaning back in the armchair. The more her eyes moved, the quicker her breaths. She grabbed my hand. Her chin dropped. "You aren't in any kind of trouble, are you?" Marigold whispered.

"Oh my word, no. No!" I laughed and felt the blush ignite up my neck to my ears. "It's not anything like that."

"Well, thank goodness for that. I'd hate to see what MamaBear would do to this nice young man." She winked at Corbin.

"A couple of months ago, you told me to mind my own business."

"Yes, I remember."

Here went nothing. "I didn't."

"Figured as much, Victoria Grace."

"Can I show you what I found? I know what day it is and what you lost a long time ago. That's why I want to show you this." I turned the laptop around to show her a portion of the Olson family tree, with the six children's names. "Here you all are. Up here is your mom and dad. All of the dates are filled in, except yours."

I slowly clicked through children, starting with baby Thomas and working backwards. "The information you found before was correct. They all died of pneumonia or complications, within six months of each other."

Tears zigged down the wrinkles on Marigold's cheeks. She reached out, and I held the screen for her to touch. Resting her fingers on each name, she paused at her mother's. "Where is Daisy?"

My heart thunderclapped. "She's right here." With a click, Daisy's tree spread across and down the screen. "She left Manazar Camp on November 21, 1945, married, and had six children. Her first daughter was named after you." I placed my computer onto her lap and sat back.

"Amazing," she whispered.

"Now for the best part."

Marigold looked over the top of the screen. "There's more?"

"I got ahold of Daisy's granddaughter by email. I'm waiting to hear back from her, but we'd like to set up a video chat, if you're up to it."

Her voice caught in her throat and was interrupted by coughing. I raised the bed, and Corbin got a fresh glass of water. "You sure do beat all, Victoria Grace." A silent tear tracked down her pale cheek, past the canula. "I can't believe you did this for me."

My heart squeezed so tightly that I could barely answer. "I'd do anything for you."

Marigold's eyes closed. The hand closest to me slid toward me, palm up. I pressed my hand into hers. Her breathing slowed, evening out. She'd fallen asleep, short puffs of oxygen echoing into the room.

"We should go." Corbin stood and slid his hand to the back of my neck. "I gotta get started on my Lit paper for finals."

I scrunched my nose. "Yeah, me too."

Marigold blinked awake. She looked at the laptop, kissed her fingertips, and pressed them to the screen. "I can't wait to meet my family."

———— ◦ ————

Patricia responded the next morning, and I sent my phone number and a link to the article. Figured she'd like to see her great-aunt as much as Marigold wanted to see her.

The finals crush hit Tuesday, a tidal wave of study guides and assignments. Mr. Hammond caught me on the way into class. "I forgot to tell you yesterday, but I saw your interview on Sunday evening." I wished he'd quit talking loudly. Or stop talking, period. "I also reviewed the article online and decided to give you extra credit points."

It'd mean B to an A minus. I'd take it. "Thanks."

At lunch, I guarded my pretzels from the Texan at my elbow. "I'm going to study at Marigold's."

"Today?"

"From now on. MamaBear said it was okay."

Corbin squeezed my knee under the table and grabbed a pretzel. "I'm your taxi?"

"If we could find a car, I wouldn't need to hitchhike." I leaned my head onto his shoulder. "I can ride my bike or walk. My rain jacket will keep me dry."

I felt his lips barely touch my hair. "I'll give you a ride, you big baby. Wouldn't want you to melt." He sat back up, launching into his sandwich.

"At least you acknowledge my delicate nature."

"Right. My delicate stick of dynamite."

My elbow connected with his ribcage. "Watch it, bub."

Later, with Grammy's permission, we headed over to Marigold's to study. Between subjects, we pushed sequins into the foam balls and Corbin folded origami newspaper stars. The nurses brought in extra dinner trays, and the food underneath was surprisingly tasty.

My phone dinged when I was licking the last of my pudding off my spoon.

Unknown: Hi. It's Patricia.

I held up my phone. "It's Daisy's granddaughter, Patricia." Corbin and Marigold looked at my phone. For their convenience, I read my response out loud as I typed it.

Hello, Patricia. I'm here with Marigold, studying for my finals.

Little bubbles trotted across my screen. "She's still typing." When the response popped up, I read it loudly.

Patricia: My cousin Kate is with me.

Corbin sat forward on the bed, near Marigold's feet. Behind him, Marigold cleared her throat and put her ornament down. She reached up and smoothed down her hair, hand shaking.

If you want to, Marigold is up for a video call.

I looked from my phone to my antique friend. "I'm so nervous," she whispered, flattening her hair again.

"So am I." Moving to her bed, I barely fit my rear end onto the side without falling off.

My phone lit up: Incoming Call. I held onto the phone with one hand and Marigold with the other.

Two brunettes appeared on my phone with a swipe of my finger. "Hi, Tori. I'm Patricia." Her hair was pulled back into a bun, and she had on a bright blue shirt.

The other lady waved. "I'm Kate." With hair cropped at their shoulders, it was easy to see they were related in the shape of their faces and eyes.

"Hi." I leaned into the pillow next to Marigold and swiveled the phone. "This is your Aunt Marigold."

Across the distance, both women cried and smiled, along with their great-aunt. I moved the camera to take me from the screen. I felt like a kid opening her favorite toy at Christmas.

When my arm cramped, Corbin held the phone for me. The "girls," as Marigold called them, lived in Minnesota, only a block away from each other. They held up pictures for Marigold: black-and-white stills of Daisy with her kids, Daisy at the beach, Daisy surrounded by her family at Christmas.

"Aunt Marigold?" Patricia folded the last photo down. "She always believed that you had made it out of the country and were happy. You were the bedtime stories she'd make up, about Aunt Marigold sailing away on a boat and catching a train in London."

Marigold clasped her hand to her heart. "Although I wish I could have seen her again, you both have brought me such joy." She wiped her tears with a wadded tissue. "I can't wait to talk to you again, my girls." She waved to the camera and blew a kiss.

The call beeped and dropped to a black screen. I took the phone from Corbin. MamaBear wanted to know when I was coming home. I tried to get the story across in small texts as I cleaned up my homework.

"Victoria Grace." I stopped pushing books into my backpack. Marigold held out her hand to me, and I moved to take it. "The next time I tell you to mind your own business, I hope you are every bit as stubborn. Thank you."

I leaned into her embrace. "You're welcome."

My phone growled again. Leave me alone. Ugh.

MamaBear: Have you left yet?

Walking out now.

"Busted?" Corbin held the front door open.

"She keeps asking if I've left yet."

"And there she is."

I felt my eyebrows dip and my nose scrunch when I saw her car parked next to his. How annoying. She was spying on me. "Why is she here?"

"Maybe it's a good thing," he said.

"Maybe she's mental."

His hand pressed into the small of my back. "Apple didn't fall far from that tree." I didn't need to see it, but I could hear the smile in his voice as he opened the passenger door. "Hey, Mrs.... uh, MamaBear."

She laughed under the dome light. "Close enough. Get in kid. We gotta get."

"Bye." I slipped into her car, knowing the kiss I wanted would never happen in front of my mom. Besides, that'd be awkward. She'd tease me for days. "Where are we going?"

"Can't tell you. It's a surprise."

"Are we going to look at a car?" MamaBear reached forward and pushed the volume on the radio up one notch. "A Mustang?"

The more questions I asked, the louder she turned up the stereo. I lost track of where we were as the city street lights thinned. In a dim area between an unlit mailbox and a gas station, we turned into a driveway.

The headlights of her car glared against the white house, with an overgrown rosebush to the left and garish mauve curtains glowing through a light inside. She cut the engine, but the headlights stayed on.

"Are we visiting a crime scene?" It was quiet and dark. I only knew there were houses on either side by their porch lights and driveways illuminated by solar lights.

"Nope." She got out and I followed.

It wasn't exactly quiet. There were crickets, and a car would periodically drive by. It wasn't as noisy as the apartment. There weren't television sounds coming through the walls. Kinda creepy. Exactly the type of place a creeper would jump out of the dark and make me scream like a little girl.

"What do you think?" she asked.

"That you're going to leave me here to be murdered."

MamaBear held up a key in the air. "We'll have to install a security system to make you feel better."

My brain felt like a movie where all of the oxygen is sucked out of the spaceship. "What?"

"Welcome home, Tor. It's our house!" She steered me by my shoulders to the front door. "Go on."

My key worked. Inside, a few boxes were stacked on the kitchen counter. It smelled like fresh paint. There was a ladder, our ladder, in the kitchen near the ceiling light. I turned around. "Are you serious?"

"As a heart attack, kid."

With a whoop, I tore through both of the bedrooms. "I have my own bathroom," I yelled from the little gray room.

"There's a backyard, too." I joined MamaBear at the sliding glass door near the kitchen. A crazy, bright spotlight illuminated the patchy grass. And a kennel with the plastic tags still attached.

"You got the K9 spot?"

"Well, the budget has to pass, but I'm in."

I jumped up into her arms. "Can we spend the night? Please, please, please?"

She laughed and dropped my feet back to the floor. "Sure. We'll need to go get sleeping bags. I could only pack so much without you noticing."

I pulled the top of the closest box open. Dishes. We preferred paper plates.

"Oh." She checked her phone. "I almost forgot to tell you to check your closet."

My feet couldn't get me to the only unpainted room in the house quick enough. In the open closet, I spied a large shoebox with a bow. Not one to delay, I flung off the lid.

Teeny, tiny origami stars threaded together on strings, each wrapped in tissue paper, filled the box. Carefully, slowly, I removed each cluster. At the bottom, a row of gray X-wing and black tie-fighters folded with amazing precision. Tucked under it all, a flat piece of white paper:

Thought this might improve the place.

What a toad! He knew about the house before I did and didn't tell me.

"That boy is crafty." MamaBear leaned on the doorframe. "Let's go grab some clothes."

I tucked my stars into the box again and took it with us back to the apartment. My overnight bag ended up with more than a week's worth of clothes. I never wanted to come back. And I couldn't wait to see it in the morning.

"You about ready?" I heard MamaBear jerk open the apartment door.

"Wait." I ran back to the kitchen and rummaged through the junk drawer. Found the box of tacks.

"Aren't you going to paint your room first?"

"Yeah, but I need these now." I balanced the shoebox, tacks, sleeping bag, and my pillow. It'd be worth the sore back to sleep on the floor.

When MamaBear pulled into the garage on our trip back, I

couldn't see the overgrown rosebush under my bedroom window or the funky pink curtains. But the bare porch bulb lit up our new address. And in a few months, I probably wouldn't remember having to run to the laundry room because the landlord was pounding on the door after I'd left a load in the washer.

MamaBear double-checked the door locks and I went to my room—my own very-first-house-bedroom. I dropped my loot on the floor and dragged the ladder from the dining room back to my bedroom. In the kitchen, I heard MamaBear unpack the dishes.

Tack after tack, I pinned my stars onto the ceiling. I eyeballed the gaps and added my X-wings and tie-fighters. By the time I'd finished, my thighs felt like Coach Neems had made me run up and down the bleachers twenty times.

I collapsed onto my rolled up sleeping bag and pushed the ladder back with my feet. The angle of my phone camera almost got them all in the frame.

First thing up in my room. Love it. And you.

My finger hovered over the send button. I hadn't said it yet. Seemed like an excuse to send it via text instead of in person. I sent the message before I talked myself into erasing it.

Swan dive into the deep end of love with a cowboy jock. Oh, the irony.

Twenty-Five

MR. BOLT HAD NO PLACE IN MY SCHEDULE, WHICH WAS crammed with painting over the apple green walls in my new bedroom, studying for finals at Marigold's, shuttling stuff from the apartment to the house, and trying not to explode like a geek at a Star Trek convention when Corbin would repeat that he loved me. But my former boss made sure to say hello at the hardware store when I picked out an extension cord for Marigold's tree.

More often, I watched Marigold's chest move up and down as she slept. And she slept more often than not. Her skinny legs ballooned—fluid retention, Sheila explained. Meals were mostly turned away, and she only ate a few bites when I begged.

Still, she worked on her sequined ornaments. Corbin loaded a video chat app onto her tablet so she could take calls from Patricia or Kate herself. He even bought her a lap pillow to hold the tablet upright.

The Wednesday before Christmas break, I tiptoed past the end of the bed when I heard both girls laughing from a video call with their aunt. Corbin was at a doctor's appointment. I desperately needed to cram for Chemistry. If I went to the apartment, I'd pack. And if I went to the house, I'd unpack, rearrange stuff, or search the internet for room inspirations.

"Victoria Grace, come say hello."

I ducked to her bedside and waved.

"We were telling Aunt Marigold that we will be out on January first." Patricia held up a printed paper. "Our kids will still be on break. That way, we can be there for a few days and still make it back before school starts."

Wow. That sounded expensive. "All of you are coming?"

Kate laughed. "Not all of us. My two oldest will both be in Florida with their father. But I'll have my youngest daughter with me."

"And I'll have my two youngest and my hubby. My oldest two are at college and have to work through the holidays," Patricia added.

"I can help with transportation or whatever you need." I had no idea why I offered, but I wanted to be helpful. The last car I'd looked at sold before we arrived. I'd have to see about borrowing MamaBear's car or maybe she would rent a van. This was going to be fantastic! I could see about reserving a room at a restaurant for dinner one night and taking Marigold out in a wheelchair.

"Already handled, sweetheart," Patricia said. "But thanks for the offer."

I could hear the puffs of air through Marigold's canula. She was blinking in fast spurts and her shoulders sagged.

"Auntie, I see you falling asleep, so Kate and I will sign off. Love you and I'll talk to you tomorrow."

Marigold's smile barely lifted the corners of her lips. She stopped me when I tried to move the tablet. "Can you put on music, please?"

Once the headphones nested onto her ears, I lowered the bed slightly. Lowering it all the way would make her cough. Her eyes were already closed.

Chemistry notes and equations and numbers started resembling blah, blah, blah after an hour.

How goes the appt?

Corbin: Double booked. How's M?

I looked up. Beneath the blue flowers of the comforter, her belly bulged.

She's okay.

My brain hissed at the lie.

———┤ • ├———

"You think I don't notice you working on my ornaments, young man, but I know." Marigold's snowy eyebrow twitched with her smile.

"Caught me, Miss Marigold." He twisted the last one in the air for her to see. "Almost done." The lights bounced off the wave-patterned blood-red and clear sequins. "Would you like to do the honors of finishing the last bit here?"

She pushed the final three pins in and told Corbin where to hang it on the tree. "Victoria Grace, would you go see what is on the menu tonight?"

"Uh, sure?" Rather than ask why she needed to know, I slid my phone in my pocket and walked to the cafeteria to see the posted menu. Turkey and mashed potatoes. Of course I was staying. Yum.

"It's turkey and…" I turned the corner into the room. "Mashed potatoes." Corbin was sitting near her waist, holding her hand, tears brimming when he turned his face to me.

"Good." Marigold cleared her throat and shifted her bed more upright. "That means you'll stay because it's your favorite."

What was going on?

"I'm glad we got the tree done before Christmas." She smoothed the comforter when Corbin stood and walked by me, into the hall.

"Yeah." I watched him disappear around a corner. "Me too."

"And our soldiers should be getting their packages soon. Only two more days until Christmas."

"I thought we might hear back from one or two of them."

"For shame, Victoria Grace." Her words snapped my wandering mind right back into the room. "We wrote for them, not for us."

I grunted. "You're right."

"Of course I am."

———┤ • ├———

There wasn't much discussion about where we'd spend Christmas Day. MamaBear was off, but offered to work four hours early in the morning for another officer so he could have time with his family.

It'd been a miracle that I finally thought of a gift for Corbin. I didn't want to be too serious or cheesy, so I wrapped a pair of foam swords, for an epic battle, and a new beanie. I'd already stolen two.

Marigold threatened to talk about underwear in front of Corbin if I bought her a gift. I gambled and found little yellow and orange paper flowers. Strung together on a long cord, they looked like a marigold wedding garland from India that I'd seen online.

A practical type of gal, I bought MamaBear new silverware. Ours was a mismatched collection. And Grammy would get a gift certificate for a pedicure because I really had no idea what to get her.

I arrived early at Willow Springs, as requested, courtesy of my personal, hot taxi driver, who then returned to his house to have Christmas morning with Aunt Sue. Marigold asked me to help arrange her gifts on the table under the tree. Then we slipped a red cashmere sweater onto her arms.

"I've never felt cashmere before." I straightened her collar. It was like petting a cloud.

"Paris. 1967. They had the best clothing."

I brushed her hair and blotted on a bit of pink lipstick.

Grammy and Corbin arrived first, with food. MamaBear came after her shift, still in her black long-sleeved shirt, uniform pants, and boots. Once we were stuffed from pot roast, red potatoes, and a yummy fruit-and-whipped-cream creation, Marigold insisted on presents.

Gratefully, Marigold did not mention underwear and asked me to hang the garland on the cupboards, where she could see it. MamaBear was happy that we wouldn't come across as slobs when people came over for dinner. Grammy was delighted—she'd never had a pedicure and made me promise to go with her.

Corbin challenged me to a sword fight after the foam hilts were uncovered. I made him wait until another day. He casually reached into his pocket and handed me a tiny box.

The type of box that has jewelry.

A ring box.

I swallowed hard. I'm not even sure if I was breathing when I flipped the top up.

The entire room laughed when I saw the curled up headphones. They all knew!

"You jerkface." I uncoiled the wires and put the half-moon-shaped buds into my ears.

Corbin grinned and took the box. "Smaller fit for your tiny ears."

"I can't hear you."

Marigold asked Corbin to hand out envelopes before giving instructions. "For my gift, I'd like you all to give what is in your envelope to a charity or someone in need. You can look if you'd like." She paused and no one moved. "You've been such a blessing to me and I'd like you to be able to bless others."

Mine was going to buy stuff for our next letter writing campaign. Send the guys and gals Easter candy. An egg hunt in the desert.

When Marigold nodded off, we tried to quietly gather everything and leave.

"Victoria Grace." I peeked over my shoulder, and she crooked her finger at me. "I'd like you to take my picture on the dresser."

"I don't want to. It's yours."

"Child, I'm tired of looking at myself. Hold onto it until the girls come out next week."

"Oh, okay." I leaned over and kissed her forehead. "Merry Christmas, Marigold."

"Merry Christmas, my child. I do love you."

———— ◦ ————

When MamaBear woke me the next morning, she didn't even have to speak. Tears spilled over her swollen red eyes, and she gathered me into her arms.

My chest burned. I'd just seen Marigold a few hours ago. She couldn't be...

The wail that tore from my throat was the only thing I could think of to take the pressure away from my heart. If I screamed loud enough, if I cried long enough, I could see her propped up in the bed, sassing me about my nose ring or correcting my posture.

MamaBear let me lie back down and covered me with blankets. I wanted my magic comforter. I wanted Marigold.

Big, strong hands stroked my hair later, after MamaBear left me crying on my pillow. I sat up and stared at Corbin. "I'm so sorry, Tor," he whispered. He held onto me until I fell asleep. And I stayed in bed the rest of the day, waiting to wake up and have everything be wonderful again. Even Trio curled up at my feet to try and help me.

Sunday, I skipped church. MamaBear was up earlier than her shift. She loaded me into the car, and we silently drove to Willow Springs. I couldn't stop the sobs when she parked.

When I worked up the courage, she held my hand tightly as we walked down the hallway to Marigold's room. Someone had unplugged her diffuser, and the stagnant smell crept in. The lights in the window had disappeared, along with the tree. My rage boiled. How dare they?

I jumped when a hand touched my shoulder from behind. It was Sheila, grief in her teary eyes. "Everything is here." She pointed, and I saw boxes stacked in the corner. "I wanted to make sure…" Sheila paused again and dropped her head. Her shoulders bounced. She sniffed and looked at me again, fresh tears dragging down her cheeks. "She wrote this after you left on Friday."

It was on our stationery, a single paper folded in half. My hands shook when I revealed her slanted cursive.

> *Victoria Grace,*
>   *Be nosy. Write to our boys. Love God and treat*
> *your boy right. My love to you, always.*
>   *Marigold*

I turned into MamaBear's shoulder and wept.

———— ⊣ ∘ ⊢ ————

Patricia, Kate, and their family's visit was a far less happy occasion than they'd originally planned. Instead of hugging their aunt, they stood next to us in the cemetery, where Marigold's ashes were interred. It was raining. That suited my mood fine.

School started again. It almost seemed like my heart was betraying her on the days I felt happy. Although I saw her picture on my dresser every morning, her voice was an echo, fading down the caves of my mind.

For a few weeks, and particularly because it was winter and raining, the days seemed grayer and more dismal.

Even though Sheila sent texts, I couldn't bring myself to visit Willow Springs. Corbin patiently talked me into stopping by. The first try, I couldn't get any further than Jamie's platinum and now pink hair before I turned into a bawling mess. The next time, Corbin held my hand and I made it down the hallway. Warren shuffled over to say hello. He told me Jasmine had succumbed to pneumonia the week before. I promised to come see him again and bring him the black licorice candy he liked the best.

The last week in January, exactly a month after Marigold had died, I found a strange envelope on the kitchen counter addressed to me. It was forwarded from our apartment and didn't have a return address. Though I knew MamaBear would be disappointed in my lack of safety by opening an anonymous letter, I haphazardly ripped it open.

> *Dear Marigold and Tori,*
>
> *Thank you for your letter. I was having a rough week, surrounded by sand instead of snow for Christmas...*

Acknowledgements

Michael. You're my favorite husband so far. There are not enough words to say how much I love you. I could quote Song of Solomon verses, but it'd get all awkward with everyone reading this.

Bean and Squish. You both fill my heart, and I'm so grateful God let me be your Mom. I'd go on and on about how you're like angels but then we'd just laugh and laugh and it's not good to lie. Let God guide your lives and don't do drugs. Or you're grounded.

Kate. Hopefully you'll buy this book. I'm glad we became friends since I had no choice about being your sister.

Dad and Mom. Thank you for feeding me and letting me read past my bedtime. I'm still bitter that you ate ice cream after I'd go to bed, though. I heard you and Jesus saw you.

Roseanna and David White. You took a chance on my first YA manuscript when I kept hearing that YA wasn't a good fit for the market. It has been a pleasure and joy to work with WhiteFire, particularly with you both, on this journey.

Rachel Kent. Still the best agent I've ever had! And answerer of my random emails. Thank you for believing in my voice and putting my story out there.

Hannah Prewett. Cinderella to my Maleficent. Unicorn to my dragon. Glitter to my goth. Eternally grateful for our friendship and your willingness to let me bounce insane ideas and sentence structures off of you.

Rosemary Johnson. Editor of my commas who reminds me to find joy. Keep making those big decisions, yes? Also, happy ones. And ones that involve buying groceries.

Amy McMaster and Robert Henslin. Without you, this magnificent cover wouldn't be possible. Thank you! Artist friends are the best. And they don't mind photoshoots in bedrooms or nine thousand cover changes.

My fabulous launch team: Jebraun, Tall Hannah, Hannah, Rhia (not her real name because she's a ninja), Amelia, Audrey, Lilah, Rosemary, and the lone dude Nate. My personal rock stars! Thank you for your support and time invested into VGJF. Without you, I'd be a sad author with no team. Go team!

For that editor who said I couldn't write Young Adult fiction. Here you go.

Tyler Joseph. Sorry I had to crease your face for my book, fren.

And reader? Don't be afraid to dream big! God created platypuses. He certainly designed a future for you.

YOU MAY ALSO ENJOY

Gone Too Soon
by Melody Carlson

An icy road. A car crash.
A family changed forever.

Seeing Voices
by Olivia Smit

Skylar Brady has a plan for her life—
until an accident changes everything.

Heart of a Royal
by Hannah Currie

Everyone wants her to be their princess...
except the ones who matter most.